SOMETHING

PRETTY

SOMETHING

BEAUTIFUL

ERIC

BARNES

Outpost19 | San Francisco
outpost19.com

Copyright 2013 by Eric Barnes.
Published 2013 by Outpost19.

Barnes, Eric
        Something Pretty, Something Beautiful / Eric
        Barnes
        ISBN 9781937402525 (pbk)
        ISBN 9781937402532 (ebook)

Library of Congress Locator Number: 2013906085

OUTPOST
19

PROVOCATIVE READING
SAN FRANCISCO
NEW YORK
OUTPOST19.COM

ALSO BY ERIC BARNES

SHIMMER

ACKNOWLEDGMENTS

Portions of this book originally appeared in *Other Voices, The Northwest Review, Tampa Review, Arkansas Review/Kansas Quarterly, Stymie Magazine, The Greensboro Review, Prairie Schooner, Best American Mystery Stories 2011, Crazyhorse, The Portland Review,* and *Pacfic Review*. The author wishes to thank these publications for their guidance and support.

FOR MY BROTHER KIRK

PROLOGUE

I'm standing alone near the cars, watching some girl I thought I'd once known, some girl from back when I was a kid. From back when I still lived here in Tacoma.

And the rain's falling lightly on this girl and the others standing around in their groups, all laughing loud or leaning their heads close together for another secret drink, and for a moment I think that maybe I should hide. For a moment I'm afraid of what this girl would do if she sees me.

But already I've realized that I don't know this girl. Realize that the girl I was thinking of wouldn't be in her teens.

I mean, her life had gone on. Everyone's has.

And still I stand watching this beginning of a party I've accidentally found, the music changing to another song, music on a car stereo and a DJ on another. I find some skinny kid in a t-shirt standing to the side of the groups. Ask where they all are going. Ask if I can get a ride across town.

"Sure," this kid says happily, barely looking at me as he talks. "We're going to the huts," he says, wiping rain from his lip. "Down in the gulch."

I sit in his passenger seat, waiting to leave, the door open but my head and face inside. I'm thinking about the huts, where I'd gone to parties, too.

And as I stare out from the car, I see a few people I'd known of when I lived in Tacoma, people who I'd never met, never talked to, but who'd gone to Puget Sound High School with me. And for these ones, I think, their lives haven't changed. Twenty-one, like me, but still hanging out with teenagers, still gathering before driving to parties in the gulch.

I lived in Tacoma till I was eighteen. But it's three years since my life there ended. Almost exactly three years to the day.

And I'm riding across the city in this kid's bright Mustang, the two of us a part of a line of jacked-up Chevys and low-riding Fords, all of it looking like some Day-Glow caravan of wannabe rebels. The spray from the road rises like a gray cloud around us, the kid offering me pot and vodka but I just drink one of his beers, the radio in his car playing loud, the kid gunning the gas as we hit the waterfront drive, passing five cars, pushing us back in our seats as the dark bay and wet, abandoned saw mills turn to a blur. This kid trying to impress me, some older guy he doesn't know, whose name he hasn't even asked.

The line of cars slows on the hill through Old Town, passing the big, nice houses there, and then reaching the smaller houses on the other side of Old Town, and we've gotten within a few blocks of where my dad still lives, where my car is, so I can get on with it, get in the car and there's a reason I'm back here in Tacoma, but then I see a house with a high, chain-link fence around it, three partly unassembled cars sitting along its driveway, two German shepherds and a pit bull tied to its porch.

It's Michael Coe's uncle's house. Coe, who I'd grown up with. "Michael Coe used to have parties there," I say, quietly, and this kid turns to me, smiling. Says, "Fuck you. You didn't go to those parties, did you?" And already I'm wondering why I even mentioned it.

"No," I say. "I've just heard."

"People say Coe and the other three broke some guy's arm at a party there," the kid says. "In front of everybody."

"No," I say and I've finished my second beer and am feeling it and feeling the drive, feeling a part of this line of cars, feeling the gulch just a quarter-mile away. Remembering the kid who'd tried to steal Coe's stereo. Remembering Coe and Teddy pinning him down on the floor. Holding him tight as I broke his nose. Holding him still as Will Wilson quietly broke his arm.

"No," I say. "They all said he just tripped."

"What's your name?" this kid asks and his smile just slightly falls.

I turn to stare at him. "Walter," I say, lying to him. "Walter Mitchell."

And it is night and I am drinking inside the entrance to one of the three abandoned utility sheds people call the huts. I've come to the party. Riding that far with the kid. Just wanting to see it. Wanting to feel it again. I'm standing alone now. Standing in the dark. Seeing my hands wet with rain. Feeling water in my hair and on my scalp. Watching this group of now seventy kids and near adults circling in the light of a bonfire. Seeing the dense brush and trees on the high gulch hillside, seeing the shine of Shuster Parkway far below our ledge. Seeing the night sky lit to brown by the miles of pulp mills and port facilities and warehouses on the Tide Flats, where my dad is working at an oil refinery right then. Seeing all these things that haven't changed since I left Tacoma.

And somewhere behind my drinking too much, I know that I should never have come. Know there is no reason to relive this again. Know I have somewhere else to be. But I'm finishing my beer, filling my cup again when no one is at the keg, circling the party, watching it all from the edges.

I'm pressing the soft of my hand against the damp bark of a tree when the skinny kid I rode with runs up to me holding a big bottle of bourbon. He's pointing a finger in my face, pointing and smiling, nodding and happily saying from behind that finger, "You're Brian Porter. You are. Someone here told me."

I stare at the fire past his head, the flames four feet high. I say to him, "I don't think the fire's big enough, do you?"

"Brian Porter," he says happily, wet finger pointing, not really knowing who Brian Porter had been. Not knowing because if he did he wouldn't have pointed a finger at Brian Porter. Wouldn't have smiled in his face.

I mean, back then, a kid like this would have been too scared even to talk to me.

"My name is Kyle," I say, pushing down his

finger as I step away from the tree, carefully walking toward an old set of stairs. "And that fire's not big enough at all."

I reach the set of wooden steps with a platform and start shaking it slowly, in a moment the kid appearing next to me, rocking the stairs with me till they break free from the building and two kids from the keg come over and the four of us lift the steps, walking then running over the grassy, muddy ground.

And the kid, the driver, he's still watching me. Smiling. Waiting as if I should say something more.

And we drop the stairs onto the fire, the platform above the flames, and the three of them are starting to yell and others are yelling too and the music from some box is grinding loud near the fire and I hear people yelling and the flames from the fire are touching the lower steps, catching the old wood quickly. And I go to the driver and take the bourbon from his hands and I'm getting drunk, watching these people I'd known and didn't know, and now someone has seen me, is maybe watching me now with this smooth bottle in my hand, the alcohol burning through my mouth to my eyes, spreading warm and hot through my throat and chest. And more people are at the fire looking at these steps and I can feel the heat on my body and light on my face and I know that there in the open anyone can see me. But I just turn to this kid. I just ask him quietly, "What do you know about Brian Porter?"

This kid is nodding. Smiling. And it's a long

time, I think, before he knows what to say. "He was wild," this kid says.

And I am feeling drunk and awful and sad and I say to this kid, "He was dead. From the day Porter was born he was dead." And I drink again and the hot is everywhere, stinging mouth to watering eyes, and I turn and throw the bottle at the steps, the glass breaking and the alcohol burning blue.

"And anyway," I say, grabbing this kid's hand hard, pressing his cold fingers together and pulling him close to me, his face near mine in the light of the fire, "my name is Will Wilson."

And the kid tries hard to jerk away from me then, and his eyes are open wide and his face is sinking and I am sure that he knows who Will Wilson was. And I am sure that he knows what that meant.

And I let go of this kid and climb to the top of the platform, the flames now reaching through the boards of the steps, the gold and smoking tips wrapping around my shoes and ankles, the rain drops hissing in the heat around me. And I turn my face up to the sky, the smoke and heat rising past my arms and neck, rushing across my ears, raising my hair so that it seems to fly all around me, but I look up at the night and the dim glow from Shuster Parkway, my lips spreading slightly, teeth grinding slow, throat and chest screaming loud. Because there on the fire I like that they see me. There in the gulch I am glad to be back in Tacoma.

1 NOW
WITH KYLE
TACOMA
DRIVING AWAY
RETURNING

1   NOW

The noise of plastic bags being pulled, ripped from the stand at the end of the conveyor at the cash register near nine, plastic torn then popped as the bag boy shakes it open with his wrist, and I am remembering the PIN on my debit card, absently, a habit, watching the numbers of the purchases scroll upward on the screen, fifty, sixty, seventy dollars in groceries, readying my PIN, not the guy in the line who struggles to remember, instead going over the list in my mind, the items I was to get, sure somehow I've forgotten one.

There's too much to remember, all of it going just so fast.

But I have to get home now, have to stop first to pick up dinner, back at the house then and through dinner and clean up and homework, work then, at the computer, till late and some TV, in bed.

Eighty, ninety, ninety-five dollars in groceries.

I live in St. Louis. I am thirty-four years old.

I say these things, most days, throughout the day. Some necessary reminder of where everything has gone.

And the noise of the store, the banging bags from counters up and down this massive room, crashing carts and beeping scanners ringing up all the items and front glass doors opening suddenly, thudding along their tracks, and the just empty buzz of the lights overhead.

But no one is talking. Not a voice. Not a person in

this room, this warehouse of groceries, all in the middle of purchase, but not one person talking. Not the checkers to the buyers, not the buyers to each other.

I turn to the line behind me. Turn slowly to the counters beyond. Look down an aisle of glassed-in frozen items. Turn toward the front doors still opening, closing again, and see how nowhere is there anyone who is talking. Some moment, really, where cell phones are off and there are no couples gone shopping and no friends in line joking with one another and no children laughing even to themselves.

I turn. I turn again. No one talking. The people silent.

I keep turning in the light, slowly, looking lost, the buyer at checkout nine seeming to hesitate over a forgotten item, calculating the risk, considering the possibility of getting it before his cart is emptied, looking around, searching aisles, thinking that maybe he could run.

But I'm only looking around at the noise without voices. The rising steady noise above and around and between so many silent people. A noise that barely reaches the sounds in my own mind. The voices there, talking fast, me most of all, making lists, making plans, reliving the day of conversations and decisions and news on the radio and words from the TV, all a thunder over the voices of the people in my memories, my voice mixed in with them now as I close my eyes hard, fighting back the sounds of friends and strangers and enemies I once knew.

1 WITH KYLE

When we were little kids, like eight or nine years old, my friend Kyle and I would walk home from Sherman Elementary together collecting bottle caps and Popsicle sticks and cigarette butts. We searched the grass and the sidewalk, under bus stop benches and around paper boxes, keeping what we found in secret pockets we made in the lining of our jackets. Kyle and I would walk home in the rain, racing the cigarette butts and Popsicle sticks along the narrow streams of water in the gutters, then days or weeks later, when it was dry, we searched for the butts and sticks in the stiff, matted mess around the sewer drains.

Kyle and I were best friends.

On rainy days back at Sherman, Kyle and I built dams during recess in the dirt near the long jump pit. The rainwater ran through the pit in a shallow, foot-wide stream as it flowed along the far side of the schoolyard toward a big, iron drain. Other kids came out to make dams too, but Kyle and me were always the first there, building the main dam, a tapering arc six inches high and five feet across, leaving the other kids to make small dams and beg us to release some water.

I remember being out there in my corduroys and nylon coat, wet like everyone else. None of us wearing raincoats. It's as if it rained so much no one bothered to fight. Except Kyle. Kyle always wore one of those bright yellow slickers, curls of black hair bursting from beneath that yellow hood. Scraping more dirt toward the dam with his yellow rubber boots.

And as recess went on and our dam got to be seven and eight inches high at the front, now ten feet around, the kids below would always start their real loud yelling, wanting us to break our dam, to let the water rush down and wreck theirs. But Kyle and me always held out, even when one of the kids tried to kick a hole in our dam – one of the hyper-active kids, usually, the ones that every day had to go to the nurse's office to take their medication. The ones like Michael Coe, who we weren't friends with then and didn't ever want to have to talk to.

I had to push Coe away once, after he tried to kick at our dam. He was a low, heavy kid with a buzz cut and tight t-shirts. I knocked him into a small mud puddle and he went into this frenzy, whipping himself in circles and screaming and his face turning red. Coe told on me, and the teacher made us put our desks together for a week, and that, we always said, is how we became friends. Although, really, that is how Coe started follow-ing Kyle and me to my house after school, show-ing up uninvited when me and my baby-sitter and the neighbor boy Teddy were playing Wiffle bat baseball or eating bologna sandwiches. How, after a while, Coe started bringing his new friend Will Wilson over to my house.

But on those rainy days in the dirt, when the bell to end recess would finally ring, on those days Kyle would only then begin to smile, carefully moving to the very front of our big dam, the other kids now yelling happily and jumping up and down and Coe and the hyperactive ones turning in fast circles, flailing their bodies onto the hard, wet ground, the teachers a hundred yards away, screaming at us from the dry doorways, and Kyle with the tip of his round, brightly booted yellow foot, he'd make just a nick in the dirt of our dam and the water would begin to trickle out.

And Coe and the other hyper ones would be breaking their thin, little dams even before the water had reached them, the water flowing faster through the now bigger break in ours, Kyle pacing back and forth, staring and watching and smiling.

And sometimes I thought I wanted to smash the wall of our dam, jump on it with my wet sneakers and let the water rush down. But I never did that to Kyle.

And now I remember a day when I looked past the kids around us, seeing some new kid leaning against the high chain-link fence, watching us all and smiling too. Smiling like Kyle was. Smiling like he understood something more. Although now, when I think of him, I think of Will Wilson in that first moment with a lean face, older, eighteen, not eight.

Will Wilson did look young then, I know. He'd been just a child. But I can't remember that so well.

But I remember standing next to Kyle, so satisfied with him. Kyle, my best friend, dry beneath his coat, me wet and warm in the rain, both of us watching our dam in the schoolyard, smiling as it went through its slow self-destruction.

•

He'd come running down the street, trying hard. He'd be running like a machine but like an old machine, not smooth, just working hard. It'd be in the evening, the man jogging on the Skyline Circle Road past the tall, leafy maples, trees that were bare in the winter, not like most of the green, tall trees there in Tacoma. He'd be running down the street faster and faster and coming toward us at the monument with the grass where we'd be playing football. He'd be sprinting then under the trees with the red and yellow or green leaves and the dark, black branches. He'd be sprinting past the big white houses on this side of the block, the side where he lived and Trevor Meyer lived.

And always Kyle would be throwing a perfect pass to somebody and I'd be getting knocked down by Trevor Meyer.

He'd be breathing hard toward us, smiling now, his feet slapping flat on the pavement. Then he'd raise his arms. And every time we'd stop playing. A year and a half it went on, back when we were eight, and lived on Stevens. On Stevens there was football in the snow, baseball in the hot clear sun, and always this jogger would be running by us, arms raised, smiling, watching us. Finally he'd stop, hands still up, looking at us all. "Just like the Olympics, huh boys?" he'd say.

I'd watch him with his hair short and still parted and pushed over. Sweat was dripping from his face and he was a good looking guy, though it wasn't something I thought about at eight. He'd walk back up the street and wouldn't say anything more unless he went over to his kid John and grabbed John's shoulder lightly and he'd say to Trevor Meyer, "You're playing John a little too close. I saw. Ease up." And then he'd smile at them both.

And then he'd walk away, arms again raised, and I'd be looking at his arms up and thinking he was pretty funny.

A funny man, I'd think.

Trevor Meyer would jump into the street then and raise his arms and run with his knees very high and his round face smiling and blonde hair bouncing and he'd say every time like Trevor Meyer did everything the same every time, "Just like the Olympics, huh boys?" and all the other people there at the circle would laugh and even John, I'd be thinking, you know, even his son John.

Only Kyle didn't laugh. Kyle just got us started playing football again.

And later we'd go back to my house, the duplex on the other side of the block, just me and Kyle and John, and my dad would be gone working. We'd get some soda crackers from the kitchen and go down the narrow stairs to the basement and watch the small TV. And always, a few minutes later, Trevor Meyer would show up.

I can remember one time when we were watching and some woman came on the TV, some commercial after the cartoon. The four of us were sitting on that round rug made of the one long, curled up, quilt-like heavy cord. The rug was hard but it was better than touching the cold concrete floor.

Trevor Meyer was saying, "They were doing it again, Kyle. I was just walking in the house and I opened the door to their bedroom to go watch cable and they were standing there naked and kissing."

Trevor Meyer was laughing and Kyle was laughing a little. But I couldn't picture them standing there naked, the Meyers. I had seen them together in their car but I couldn't picture them kissing. I tried to think of Trevor's mom kissing someone and that was hard to see. I tried to imagine her, Mrs. Meyer with her curled and frosted hair, but now with no clothes on. But I couldn't do it. I was thinking of the time when Kyle's dad was in town and he took us to the Elks Club to go swimming and he and Kyle did dives off the high dive but I just watched, Kyle doing them so well, his dad standing near me and touching me on the arm and pointing up to Kyle as he waited to climb the ladder for his turn. But in the locker room nobody was wearing clothes, there after we'd been swimming for the afternoon, me and Kyle and his dad, and there were these fat men with tight, hanging stomachs like huge watermelons all sitting in these red lawn chairs in that wet, smelly locker room. They were sitting with the hairy melon stomachs folded out to their thighs, almost their knees, and drinking plastic cups of beer or wandering across the damp concrete floor from the lockers to chairs to showers, walking slowly to the small bar, and why they stayed in there I didn't know but Kyle's dad too, he wasn't fat, but he sat like the others, cross-legged and naked in one of those chairs, reading a newspaper and drinking scotch from a paper cup.

"So I stand there," Trevor Meyer was saying, "and he yells loud, 'Get the hell out of here!' And he pushes the door and wham –" Trevor Meyer was laughing and Kyle was laughing a little and John was starting to laugh, "– it smacks me in the forehead and I fall back into the hall."

And I wondered how much it hurt and how could his dad do that and I think of my dad, but it's not like he'd ever knock me down.

"They're assholes," Trevor Meyer said and he looked at the TV and then turned to me. "What do you think they were doing?" he asked me.

I looked at him and thought, *I know what they were doing*, but I didn't know how to say it.

And Kyle was looking at the rug, pulling a dirty thread from the cord, imagining, I'd bet now, trying but not imagining what the Meyers looked like naked and were doing naked because I know now that John and Kyle didn't understand either, eight years old, all of us, but they didn't say so to Trevor Meyer because Trevor was Trevor. Instead, they knew you just nodded along. But it would be years before I learned that.

"You don't know," Trevor Meyer was saying.

I looked and saw John smiling. He was looking at Trevor Meyer and smiling.

"I know," I said but I felt it, felt the knot, like cold light spreading through my chest, suddenly there like it's always been there and will never go away.

"You don't know," Trevor Meyer was saying.

I thought, *I know*, and what if I say it, then I say it and it's wrong and it's worse and what's there, the spreading dread and the fear of being embarrassed and the feeling that this doesn't have to happen will all come out like it always comes out and so I say nothing. And that's worse. And so it was coming out anyway.

"I know," I said.

Trevor Meyer was close to me now, leaning close and his face near mine with the yellow crackers in his chalky white teeth and he was breathing and watching and waiting.

God he knows, I thought, he always knows that if he looks and stares and gets close and waits, he knows it'll come.

John was smiling and looking at me now and laughing now. And it was out and in my face and here and hot and I was like always crying and I wanted to say I'd been swimming at the Elks but all I could say was, "Screw you, Trevor."

"Oh," he'd say, smiling and Kyle would be looking down at the floor then and John, who moved with his family a year later and I never saw him again, he was smiling behind Trevor Meyer and watching too and smiling.

And it'd be over me and through me and I'd

be crying. And Trevor Meyer'd be laughing hard. "Oh," he'd say. "Oh."

John'd say, "I'm going now," and he'd be getting up and I'd be saying, "Screw you, Trevor."

Trevor Meyer would be saying, "Screw you, Trevor."

I'd want to grab Trevor Meyer but couldn't. Because if I could have known back then that crying and wanting so bad to grab Trevor Meyer and shake him and press his face against the floor, the wanting John to stop laughing when I'd hear him say, "I'll see you later," and wanting it all to stop, the spreading and the hot, wanting someone to stop it, if I'd known like I know now that this all was nothing, then I'd have been in Trevor Meyer's face, looking on at him and casting him away, not wasting my time, not caring one bit. Standing cool and quiet like Kyle when we were kids.

But instead I'd watch Trevor Meyer run around that basement room, hands in the air, yelling, "Just like the Olympics, huh boys?"

And I'd be hitting the floor, crying.

"Naked again," Trevor Meyer would be saying, running in his circles. "They're little sex Olympics," he'd say, smiling and laughing hard. Running in a circle still, running as I cried and wished I could have stopped him and answered him right. Cried as I knew that wouldn't happen. Even as I knew that wasn't the answer.

And Trevor, he'd still be running, hands in the air, laughing, sometimes laughing hard like that for half an hour or an hour, sprinting around the basement, swinging his hands in the air.

Until finally Kyle would stand and he'd make Trevor stop. Would make Trevor sit. Would make Trevor say he was sorry.

And Trevor would leave. And Kyle and I would watch some more TV and play with my trucks and he'd never once mention how I had cried.

•

By the time we were twelve, Kyle was already one of those hairy people. One of those people with just one long, deeply overgrown eyebrow that reaches not just across his forehead but, if you looked real close, it reached down the sides of his face, crawling its way toward his ears.

Kyle was also one of those people who gets naked, hairy even at twelve, his hands and arms already forever stained green gray with the fish slime and engine oil from working on his uncle's fishing boat.

I don't know why Kyle got naked so often. I think it was just his way.

Kyle was standing at the microwave this day, watching an egg turning slowly on the plate, his face only an inch from the humming black box. "Just wait," he kept saying. "Here it comes, just wait."

Kyle had come by my house to blow up an egg in the microwave. He was naked.

"How about some clothes then?" I said to

him, standing in the doorway to the kitchen. Not getting too close.

But he only kept saying, "Just wait, just wait."

I started to say something about clothes again, but the egg popped loudly, and Kyle exploded in silent laughter. "My god," he was saying, barely making noise in his laughing, "my god," and he couldn't stop laughing.

I was shaking my head at him. "You're cleaning it all up," I said.

"Another one," he was saying. "Please. Just hand me one more egg."

He was pulling open the microwave door with one hand, with the other opening the fridge.

Kyle's family didn't have a microwave. They just didn't see a need. It was something about spending so much time on fishing boats, cooking full meals for crews of eight on a two-burner propane stove.

My dad had just won this microwave in a bet.

Kyle was nodding, putting two eggs in the microwave now. He fumbled a little trying to turn it on.

"So why are you naked?" I asked him.

His face was against the microwave door. The plate inside was turning again. "Clothes got wet."

"How?" I asked.

"Spilled something."

"What?"

The microwave still buzzed, the two eggs turning steadily in front of him. "Spilled something," he said. "On the way over here."

"What did you spill?"

"Huh?" he said.

"What did you spill on your clothes?"

"Oh," he said, "right. Eggs."

The two eggs popped, one then the second, Kyle jumping back from the microwave and laughing his silent laugh, leaning against the counter, that easiest happiest airy laugh.

"I've always wanted to do this," he said.

"You spilled eggs?" I asked loudly, still hoping for an answer.

He was trying to talk again, trying to stop his laughing, to get out his words. "Yes," he said. "Eggs," he said. "I was bringing eggs here to blow them up."

•

When we were thirteen, I'd go out on Puget Sound with Kyle in a ten-foot dinghy we'd rent from the park at Point Defiance. You could rent little 20 horse motors to put on the back of the boats and we'd go out in the winter in three layers of sweatshirts, heading along the edges of the city and the port, cruising the shores for things that might have gotten loose from a boat or ship. Kyle's dad had told him once that as a kid he'd every week take a rowboat out into Puget Sound off Tacoma and search for logs that had broken free from their rafts, these huge flat rafts of hundreds of logs that were brought down the rivers from the forests inland. When he found a log, he'd snag it with a steel hook and a rope and pull it to the mill, where they'd give him a few dollars for it.

Kyle's dad had been a logger and a fisherman and a hand on his family's fishing boats. He'd worked on the railroad and he'd worked as a truck driver bringing cement to a couple of the dams built on the Columbia River. He'd spent summers on farms all over eastern Washington and eastern Oregon. He was sixty when Kyle had been born and seventy when he died. He'd lived in Alaska for most of Kyle's life and was hit by a car there, driving to the store near the docks where he kept his boat, and the car that hit him had blown through a light, midday, going way too fast. Kyle's dad was a nice guy, I remembered, who could make anything and fix anything and who once picked me up into the back of his truck and it felt like he could have thrown me fifty feet. I felt like nothing in his hands.

The log rafts were still brought down to Puget Sound from the Puyallup River when Kyle and I were kids renting those dinghies. The tugs floated them out into the bay and pulled them over to the mill at the tip of one of all those manmade peninsulas at the port. But it was different, Kyle and I thought. The mill, the oil refinery, the ships loaded and unloaded with containers from all over the world. They were automation jobs, worked by kids who'd been in vocational school since they were teenagers, learning computers and practicing their math.

I was thirteen and knew I didn't want a job like that. The only good job left was to fish, like Kyle's family, work that disappeared bit by bit each year that we grew older. That's what Kyle told me. Every year Slavs like Kyle and his family sold their fishing permits and fifty-year-old boats to the government, or sold out to the Indians, who a lot of Slavs didn't like because they got special privileges, special treatment like extra days when the white fisherman couldn't fish for salmon.

At thirteen I thought you could fish or you could go to Alaska and if you were lucky you could do both. There were good jobs left in Alaska, doing all kinds of things. Driving trucks along the Alaskan Highway like my dad had done, or being an oil worker up on the North Slope, or captaining a tug pulling barges to the Aleutians. Even just getting a good construction job, doing that in Alaska was better than anywhere else. It paid better and the work was outdoors and you'd be making something like a city pier in Southeast or some airport way out near Anchorage or houses up north of Fairbanks.

And at thirteen Kyle and I would rent one of those boats from the park and cruise the bay and talk about this till seven at night, when you had to turn the boats back in. We knew a lot then and were sure where we would be when we were older and while we were out on Puget Sound for the day we wouldn't find much, maybe a cooler that had blown off some pleasure boat or rubber bumpers or garbage, or some cans that had pushed up against the old piers, but it always felt good to be out.

It was Kyle who'd said that getting naked was just his way. Kyle who'd started driving to his after school job when he was twelve, using a beat up car his older cousin had given him. Kyle who would move out when he was fifteen, going to live with his aunt when it all got to be too much at his house. Kyle who would take me to Alaska when we were eighteen. Kyle who knew, from the beginning, that if you wanted to you could get out. Kyle who I remember, still, in a fight on a hill under the Proctor Bridge with Will Wilson when we were eighteen. The only fight Will Wilson ever lost.

1   TACOMA

I had other friends. Michael Coe and Ted Selva and Will Wilson. They didn't really know Kyle. I would spend time with them when Kyle was working for his uncle. It was louder with them and we moved around more and faster. And sometimes I'd be with them even when Kyle wasn't working, when he was just at his aunt's house, building things with his dad's old tools.

Coe and Teddy and Will Wilson and me, we would drive through Tacoma, fourteen years old and the windows down and feeling the warm air in summer and early fall, the cool or cold air in the winter and spring. Will Wilson driving, music I didn't know hammering quietly from the speakers under the rear window of the car, the four of us sometimes talking as we drank, maybe looking absently at the neighborhoods around us. Seeing the lit-up shopping centers and glowing supermarkets, bright asphalt parking lots and cinder block schools. Will Wilson, Michael Coe, Ted Selva and Brian Porter, all passing around wet bottles of beer. We rode along the miles of straight streets linking rows of square blocks, rows of boxed houses and shopping centers laid quickly over what had been scattered woods when I was a kid and what had been deep forest when my dad was a kid. All of it these grids. Only the new neighborhoods had curves, built on winding cul de sacs and circular drives, each filled with similar houses and built very close to each other, each winding neighborhood confined to a square, so that still in Tacoma you drove along the grids.

The four of us would drive sixty miles an hour through that simple order, crossing through those neighborhoods and the Tide Flats with its warehouses and pulp mills and oil refineries. And we'd drive along the highways circling the edges of the city.

You live your life telling stories, to people in a bar, to the guys you work with, to women you meet. When you're a kid you tell stories to each other, sometimes only killing time between the next story you'd make. Will Wilson told stories with us and now when I think about him I think that maybe he told the stories with us, about the things the four of us did, only until he got bored of them, and then he started to make a new plan, to start a new story we could later tell.

When I was twenty and in a bar or working, I would tell stories too, to the people around me, about the four of us mostly, about driving or about some fight we had or about playing car tag when we were fourteen.

There were stories I liked telling, car tag was one, and there were stories I didn't ever tell. And so even then you're telling a new story. Making up a story out of the pieces of your life you leave out.

In car tag there were two cars, each carrying

a driver and gunner, each team trying to shoot one of the other team's members with a BB gun. Car tag was supposed to be about BB guns and high speeds, but once near Point Defiance Park when we were all fourteen, Will Wilson threw three M-80s at Teddy and me, these taped together, finger-sized smoking sticks flying toward Teddy's open window.

Teddy and I were wearing green Army gas masks that Teddy had bought at one of the military surplus stores near the Fort Lewis Army base. The rubber straps were wrapped around our heads, the clear plastic fronts protecting our eyes better than the blue or red swim goggles we all usually wore. The only problem with the masks was that our voices were muffled to a whisper and each mask had a soup-can-sized air filter sticking out awkwardly from the chin.

I'd known Teddy since we were eight. Teddy had been the really nice neighbor boy, a sweet kid who I'd played with when there was nothing else to do.

And so the yellow M-80 bomb flew right through the window, landing on the seat between Teddy and me, me at the wheel of the beat up old Chrysler I had for a while. Will Wilson and Coe were speeding away in Coe's orange Ford, and Teddy and I were stopped in the middle of an intersection, looking at this bomb between us, screaming and laughing in our masks, the laughing so hard but the sound all deadened and distant and the plastic fogging up from our breath and Teddy was pawing at his door handle but he couldn't take his eyes off those M-80s. And I reached with my bare hand and slapped the M-80s into the back seat, the triple explosion right then putting three two-inch dents in the floor and blowing one of the back door's vinyl panels into the front seat between us. It also lit a fire in the upholstery, and the flames were now spreading fast, smoke pouring quickly across Teddy and me, a car behind us honking, the driver of the car next to us frantically rolling up her window. But Teddy and I hadn't moved. We were only screaming and laughing and trying to do something but mostly just laughing, the fire growing larger, flames spreading even faster up the back of the seat, me holding my ears trying to stop the ringing from the explosion, still yelling into my mask not from the fire but from the scare of those M-80s. And I saw through the windshield Coe and Will Wilson now pulling over near the intersection, out of their car, jerking forward and back as they stood and laughed, Coe in his blue swim goggles, Will Wilson in red. Will Wilson raising his gun, shooting me right in the neck.

Will Wilson, I would sometimes tell people, taking a break from playing pool in a bar in Wyoming, Will Wilson, I would tell them, could just be heartless.

Will Wilson, I would say, if I had drank enough and it was still those first few years after I left Tacoma, Will Wilson was the coldest person I have ever known.

Will Wilson, now, he never appears in the stories I tell.

But in that car in Tacoma I was laughing even harder, screaming louder as I held my neck, looking at Teddy through the fiery haze. And he was watching me through his clear plastic mask, his thin hair poking up and out from the rubber edges, smiling his kid-like round grin at me as he put his hand around the filter at his chin, chest heaving in a deep, slow breath, gray smoke covering him, swirling around his face as I heard his muffled, unnatural yell, "Hey Brian," his voice screamed quietly, "these masks really work!"

And so I talked on. In the pool hall. Or a bar. Or a pickup truck riding out to a warehouse on the edge of a ranch. Talking fast, hearing the stories of others all now starting on top of mine, and that's when you could believe that nothing else had ever happened at all.

I could tell people about driving, and about going into the gulch.

I was seven when I first went into the gulch. I was walking on the very high but only block-long Proctor Bridge and I looked over the rail and saw a slightly twisted body lying in the shadows and puddles a hundred feet down. Me and the kids in front of me were already running back to the end of the bridge where there was a small park with swings and logs to climb on, and I thought the kid had jumped or fallen and knew he wasn't alive, but didn't at all realize he'd be dead if I got to him. And I ran past the swings to the steep trails behind the park, trails that led into the gulch and I was halfway down the hill, passing into the shade of the trees now, the trail getting steeper and me sliding on my thighs and butt, the rocks from the kids behind me bouncing against my back and head and at the bottom of the hill I was almost tripping on the dusk-like dark floor, running across the mud and leaves, and above me were the tall, sweeping arches of the concrete bridge supports, and the high ledge at one end in the shadows of the bridge, and I was the first and didn't know what to do and there was the kid. A kid who'd been strangled, I found out later. By some neighborhood lady. And I touched this kid's arm, just to see what it felt like.

It felt cold, and a little hard, and a little damp.

The gulch's miles of dark trails and wet trees and bushes cut through the square neighborhoods in the North End of Tacoma, winding with no real starting place, thin and shallow offshoots leading to public parks, to wide, deep bowls that opened onto the bay. It wound through the North End without a beginning or end, some parts dropping a few hundred yards deep and reaching maybe a half mile across, others parts dropping only twenty feet deep and reaching thirty yards across. We drank and smoked in different parts of the gulch, and when we were younger played army and tag down there also. Too uneven or steep to build on, the gulch was a last remnant of untouched nature, except for the tires and broken beer bottles in it, and the few old concrete utility buildings. The buildings called the huts were near an offshoot and were used by lots of kids for parties. Other buildings were deep in the gulch and few people knew about them. The four of us played games around these sheds as kids and drank in them as teenagers.

You tell people that. How you ran through those trails for hours, all day.

And you tell people how you'd get beer. How you'd hang out in a parking lot asking someone to buy for you. Or how you stole it from your uncle. Or how you knew someone who knew someone who would buy beer for you.

When we were thirteen, after my neighbor Teddy and me had begun hanging out with Will Wilson and his big friend Coe, then the four of us would go to this longshoreman's house to get beer, some guy in his twenties, one of four or five people Will Wilson knew who would buy for us.

"Yeah, yeah," this guy would say slowly, not irritated, not happy, just nodding for us to come inside, sitting and tying his boot laces before hovering out a hand for our collected dollar bills.

But I remember other parts of getting beer. The parts you don't see a reason to tell. Remember us all sitting so quietly in the guy's house as we waited. Not talking to his wife. The five of us just watching the Friday night shows on their big TV. And I can remember glancing at the low leather couch, at the porcelain cows and owls on the glass table, at the collection of albums pressed between two wooden milk crates. I remember the pink and white net of the baby pen on the floor, remember staring for a while at the smiling daughter rolling aimlessly on the two-tone shag carpet. Remember that the wife seemed so old, though I'm sure now she was maybe twenty. And I remember looking away from that, the TV and people and especially that baby on the floor, looking past the Formica dining room table covered with fishing tackle and a hunting rifle, looking away from the house of this guy who worked on the Tide Flats, the Tide Flats where all our dads worked, where I knew I would soon start working part time and as I stared out the dining room window, I saw that there at the edge of the small backyard, pushing heavily against a high chain-link fence, there was the thick wet tangle. Again there was an entrance I'd never seen. Again there was the gulch.

And we would drive. Fifteen years old and the four of us driving eighty-five miles an hour down Sixth Avenue or Pearl, across Shuster Parkway or the Tide Flats. One night like so many nights, the four of us screaming along Shuster inside a car turned pale blue from the streetlights reaching out over the concrete road, me driving my old Impala, a car I'd bought just that week. And I took my hands from the wheel, began to pull myself through my window. My head and chest were outside when Will Wilson grabbed the wheel from the passenger seat, the car already accelerating as he hit the gas.

We did this every night, it seemed, till we were all eighteen.

I was pulling myself through the window, the tips of my fingers against the molding along the doors, Will Wilson from the passenger seat putting his hand on the wheel and his foot on the gas as my legs crossed the door frame, my chest and arms now out flat on the roof, my whole body up there, face turned to the wind, one arm hanging onto the door frame to my left and now I was yelling *now, now, now* not at Will Wilson, Coe and Teddy in the car, but at myself. I could feel my ribs against the warm steel, felt the wind cool, almost cold as it cut across my hands at eighty-five miles an hour, tearing at my face till my eyes went so blurry that I could barely see, but even in the wind I could hear the three of them screaming under me, could feel them thumping against my chest through the metal, could hear the music loud from the radio, a distorted, simple song I'd heard four times that day.

And unless the car was a Chevette or Toyota, on the roof you weren't able simply to reach over to the passenger side while holding onto the driver's side. The four of us usually bought the very inexpensive old Buicks or Pontiacs. Big, wide family cars. And so on the roof of that wide Impala, like most all the other cars we ever climbed across or would try to cross, I started to slide to the other side, letting go of the driver's side molding, pressing my hands flat against the smooth roof, feeling that I was touching very little, just hoping for the far molding, the far side, the goal. My right hand reached toward the edge, fingers extended, wind ripping at my knuckles. Moving eighty or eighty-five across the ground but on the roof you floated slowly, sliding, the car shaking under you from the speed and the wind and the friends, the three beating hard. Sliding with no grip. Sliding a little faster.

Screaming now, now, now, because that says all you could say skimming across steel toward the rear window. Guiding yourself slightly with your flat palms against the roof, trying not to fight because if you do, if you lurch or push too hard, then you'll slide backwards too fast. So you let yourself slip, drifting away from the driver's edge and toward the back, knowing that at the back there is nothing to grab, just the smooth glass and a hard bounce to the trunk and a hard bounce to the bumper and a drop to the asphalt road. We used to say that the asphalt pulled and it was drunk boys talking but on the roof you believed it. And so you floated toward that edge barely breathing at all with the waiting and trying and hoping and screaming, knowing that for your minute on the roof, you are free. Riding down Shuster, streetlights shining cold white in your eyes, reflecting so brightly off the high concrete wall along the road, feet, even knees, touching the smooth rear window. Then you are alone, no one else, no one driving, no one screaming and pounding on the roof of a car. No knowing, no future. No worries beyond that moment, no thinking beyond your timeless seconds of forever waiting, reaching, wanting to catch that edge, wanting one thing, one idea. Wanting it so bad.

Now. Now. Now.

And I grabbed that edge. Ripped on my fingers, tore at my nails, clung to the molding. Teddy lost a nail once at seventy-five, three nails once at eighty. Two of them never came back.

And I was screaming, spinning myself halfway through the back seat window, seeing Will Wilson only now sliding into the driver's seat, having driven with one foot and one hand, moving over now only because I was safe inside, now because there was no danger with everyone in the car.

And what I didn't tell anyone, later, when I'd tell the easy version of one of those moments, what I didn't tell them was how when I was back in the Impala I can only remember the screaming, all that screaming from me and them, my feet still hanging out in the cold wind along Shuster, all of us knowing the police could be avoided, parents couldn't stop this. Knowing those things didn't matter. Because as I sucked warm alcohol past the hard glass rim of a bottle, ears ringing with the noise, throat turning raw from the screams, then I knew there was no reason for this to ever end.

And so I never told anyone how one time in the rain Will Wilson rode on the roof of his car at one hundred miles an hour. A night when we were seventeen and Will Wilson brought his Plymouth up to eighty miles an hour on Shuster, turned to me in the passenger seat and smiled, said, *Come on Porter, let's go a hundred.* I slid into the driver's seat as he started his climb, had the car up to ninety as Will Wilson hit the roof. Rain shining brightly on the high wall to the left and low wall to the right. Streetlights glowing pale gold on the hood, headlights reaching forward across the pavement. Me pushing the car to ninety-five, fingers tapping the wheel as we hit a hundred. The bay to our right so dark in the night, the Browns Point lighthouse just a very distant blur. Will Wilson above us in the rain, me imagining his face steadily hit with a spray of water, his hands rubbing stiffly, jerking, then gliding easy across the wet, steel roof. And as he floated above us, Will Wilson slid toward the rear too fast and missed the passenger side windows. His body below the neck hit the trunk, his feet hanging out over the road, the car so loud with Teddy and Coe and me laughing and pounding on the car, the engine screaming on at one hundred and ten, the spray from the road turning white on the windshield, Coe screaming in my ear as he reached past me to turn up the music.

And Will Wilson did grab the edge he needed, did climb into the car. Saying when he was inside that it was beautiful. Shaking his wet hair, again and again wiping the water from his face, saying, *It was beautiful, my God, it was beautiful.*

The four of us never called anything beautiful. Especially Will Wilson. Will Wilson who led us, with the beer and pot and the girls he knew, with the way he swept his thin, hard arms at anyone in a fight. But Will Wilson that night said his ride was beautiful and no one questioned him, even mentioned it when he'd said it so many times.

"He just kept saying it," Teddy said later. "Just kept saying *beautiful*."

And after an hour Will Wilson was sitting quietly in the back seat, drinking slowly, the other three of us talking some and drinking, finally parking at the train tracks above the waterfront. Will Wilson after a few minutes getting out and standing in the rain. In a minute carefully laying down in the mud. It's the only time Will Wilson ever passed out. The three of us had to take him home laid out in the back seat, had to carry him to his garage door near the alley. Lay him carefully next to the wood pile, quietly cover him with an old plastic tarp.

For a few minutes we stood watching him, not talking. Then Teddy, Coe and I quietly drove to the Proctor Bridge, carried the rest of our beer to the high dirt ledge underneath the Proctor's tall span. Stared at the bridge's concrete supports stretching out and then down. Heard around us the low, numbing sound of the rain against the leaves.

We didn't mention Will Wilson. Our friend who'd never feared his step-dad or a fight or a car moving fast. Will Wilson who one time when we were in the gulch and Teddy said *Come on Will, no,* Will Wilson turned from what he was doing to some kid and he beat Teddy till Teddy lay in the black mud of a deep puddle, beyond crying, beyond frightened, raising his head to spit brown water and bits of dirt and blood from his already swelling face, trying lamely to wipe his eyes with his broken hand and wrist. When Teddy had spoken, Will Wilson had turned and leaned back slightly, moved toward Teddy at a speed I couldn't follow, his arms and fists striking and slashing, hard and bare and too sharp for hands.

Will Wilson made our lives. He broke down limits Coe and Teddy and me didn't want. And by the time I left Tacoma, Will Wilson had given us all the kind of purpose and power that little kids fantasize about and most adults can never quite achieve.

As we stood there on that ledge, I thought of Will Wilson near the wood pile, remembered his mouth open, eyes staring out behind half-closed lids. His usually hard face gone somehow soft. We were seventeen that night. This was in the middle of it all. I was afraid of Will Wilson and all that he could start. But that night I was most afraid that, even for a few hours, Will Wilson had left us.

Because I liked what Will Wilson brought us. Liked it very, very much.

And that night under the bridge, Coe and Teddy and I started slowly breaking bottles in the dark. Didn't plan it. Didn't talk about it. We just shared one last beer to drink, then pulled the unopened bottles from their cardboard case. Threw the heavy, brown glass at the concrete arches, felt the smooth bottles releasing from our wet fingers. Heard them flying through the dim light below the bridge, heard them breaking unseen against the dropping, then rising supports.

And I was thinking how even when Will Wilson had been on the roof, nearly falling past the trunk, the three of us hadn't believed he was in danger. We hadn't believed he could even be hurt. And I think I did see how we'd lost ourselves to him. How the worst desires in each of us had left us blind and numb.

How that numbness kept the three of us from admitting we were lost.

And the full bottles were hitting the concrete in thick, slow thuds. Eight bottles. Twelve. The sound echoing on against the ledge beneath our feet and roadway above our heads, reaching quietly through the supports before spreading down to the trees, seeming to grow even louder with each bottle we threw, finally fading slowly in the dark and darker distance of the gulch.

It was beautiful.

1 DRIVING AWAY

"Sing *Kumbaya* with me," I start saying slowly, somewhere in Idaho. "Really. Let's sing together."

Tacoma, where our trip began, is four hundred miles behind us. We are both a little sweaty. Both feeling very thick in our seats.

But we are happy.

It's later. We're twenty-one and I haven't seen Kyle in a few years.

Kyle is moaning, the sound falling and rising very quietly, forming some song of an idiot savant. His head is leaning back, his square face and jaw barely quivering. He is smiling slightly. His hair is short and curly and his bright green eyes are set almost too far back in his head.

I am driving. "Sing *Kumbaya* with me," I say again.

"I hate that song," Kyle says without force, like me glad to be lost in the dead time of the road.

Idaho is hot and dry outside the car, the broad sky spotted with a hundred identical clouds, pure white puffs that are spread like a checkerboard through the blue, casting slow-moving shadows on the gray asphalt highway and the soft waves of yellow grass around us.

In a moment, I ask Kyle, "Why do you hate *Kumbaya*?"

He doesn't answer and I don't care.

"It's just a friendly camp song," I say brightly. "A happy road song."

"It's a dumb church song, Brian," Kyle says. "It makes me want to snap my fingers in time."

We move out from beneath a shadow into the two o'clock sunlight, the road here shining almost white, the farmland blowing in slow, gold waves.

"It's a religious song?" I ask. I hadn't ever thought of that. In the car, four hundred miles into the trip, this seems to carry some importance.

"How could you not know that, Brian?" Kyle asks slowly. "Kum-ba-ya, *my Lord*," he says flatly, determined not to sing. "Kum-ba-ya. *Oh Lord*, Kum-ba-ya."

Under the sound of our voices I can hear the dim hum of the tires on the pavement.

Only Kyle has ever called me Brian. Not Porter, but Brian.

Teddy did, sometimes. But that seems different.

"We didn't have religion in my house," I say. "The neighbors had religion. Other people had religion. I'm sure if you asked him, my dad would say he believed in God. But the only time he talked about it was when I was a child and there was thunder and my dad said to me from the couch, 'The noise there, the rumble, that's just God bowling.'"

And that is the longest I've spoken in hours. In the slowdown of the road, it seems like the longest I've spoken in years.

I've drank two beers and Kyle has drank half

of one.

We near a young man and woman hitchhiking in the narrow shoulder, thumbs raised to us, the woman turning to show her round, pregnant belly under a loose dress printed with peace signs and birds. The bearded man points at her stomach, smiling as if proud of the guilt it can evoke. She leans back. His palms rotate slowly toward the sky.

Come on, man.

Kyle presses his hands against the roof, moaning loudly, and I can smell him, a strong and warm, almost bitter body scent. But a nice smell. A good smell.

The car changes lanes. I look down at my hands on the wheel.

And in the moments where all I know are the cars and fields around us, the hum of tires across the road and the sound of the music on the stereo, the warm then cool air under clouds or blue sky, then I can think about our past in Tacoma as something that is done, a set of memories to look at if I want, ignore if I choose. I can think about now, about my life working and the work I've done and the money I've made and the work I've learned, and I can believe that the future is new and unknown and wholly separate from the past.

Kyle turns to me, eyes so green. "You smell like smoke," he says. "Like a fire."

I stare at him for a moment. His hair is short like it was when we were little kids. I turn to look back at the road.

"I knew I smelled something," Kyle says. "But

I thought it was the car."

"No, no," I say, staring forward. "It's me."

I lean back into my seat. Stare out at the high-way. Seeing six brown birds flying low along the hot and blurry asphalt.

I can't mention the huts, and the fire there, to Kyle.

"It's me," I say again, and we are nearing the birds and there'd been only two of them, the others a reflection in the heat, and one pulls up suddenly, banking toward the windshield as if drawn to the car, veering across our faces in a rush of quiet, quick breaths from Kyle and me.

And I turn to watch that bird fly across the field, hoping Kyle will watch it too, hoping he'll forget about the smoke.

But in a moment he is asking. In a moment he is saying, "The fire. The smoke."

And already I am answering. Saying, "I didn't have time to shower." Saying, "A cookout. Last night. Back in Tacoma."

And already the lies have started again.

1 RETURNING

There are dreams that come, but she's stopped be-
lieving they are dreams, this whirling hurricane
just a few blocks wide, moving toward her now so
that all she can do is lower her head, step up to the
open window, and fly.

On the best days, she can fly. And on this day,
she does.

But now she wakes up in the tangled sheets of
the second bed. She is three days from Tacoma.

The room and the motel around her are quiet.
She can hear a semi down-shifting out on the interstate. She opens her eyes and pulls the sheet and
blanket away from her naked body. The gray light
from the window behind the curtain colors her skin
a pale blue. For a minute, she lays there staring
down at herself, breathing slowly.

She stands from her bed in the motel and goes
to the window. She pulls aside the curtain. Cold
air blows lightly against her bare stomach, coming
thinly from the heating unit. She stares out at the
few cars in the parking lot. A low chain-link fence
separates the lot from a half mile of flat, vacant
land that surrounds the highway for a few hundred
miles. She leans close to the glass to look at her old,
white Dart.

She hopes it hasn't been broken into. She looks

closely to see if any windows are broken. Or if a door has been jammed open.

Those things cost money, she is thinking. *Those things would take a day or two to fix*, she is thinking.

She's almost out of money. And she doesn't have any time.

She presses her hand against the cold glass. The window faces east and she can see the start of the sunrise. The sky near the horizon has turned blue and below that there is a thin, barely wavering line of gold.

She wishes again that she'd flown. But a flight from Florida would have been so expensive. *A few days won't matter,* she is thinking now.

She presses her forehead against the cold window of the motel, feels the glass numb and wet. Sees in the reflection her tangled brown hair that reaches to her shoulders, her long, still face, her dark eyes, even the room behind her, and everything inside it, all of it lit bright by the beginnings of the sunrise.

She closes her eyes and tries not to cry.

2 NOW
WITH KYLE
TACOMA
DRIVING AWAY
RETURNING

2 NOW

I go to the circus now, and always it reminds me of the B&I back in Tacoma, a large discount department store with a fake, plywood circus tent built across the front of the building. Checkout counters stacked with bags of peanuts. An indoor carousel with two-minute rides. Coin-op bucking broncos made of hard, slick plastic. Coin-op convertible sports cars that riddled your back with bruises. And behind the games, in a small room with no sign, was Ivan the Gorilla in a glassed-in cage. You could buy cheap boots at the B&I, take a ride on the carousel. You could suck in helium from balloons tied to the metal racks at the ends of every aisle and you could go to that glass wall and talk to Ivan in a high helium voice, tap on the glass till he turned from his TV and tap on the glass till he pounded on the window, pounded on his chest, pounded so hard that the floors and walls began to shake.

And I watch my kids screaming, smiling, laughing at the scene of this circus we're watching.

And I sit back. And I smile. And I close my eyes.

It's almost over. Smile some more. For the kids.

I have always hated the circus.

Smile some more.

2   WITH KYLE

The trees and brush ahead of us would come slow then fast then a blur. The road was like the bottom of a deep canal, the high trees the walls of the on-coming dark corridor. The old VW bounced hard on the narrow, dirt path, branches and leaves scraping against the hood and doors and sometimes catching inside the windows, the engine's easy drone echoing back from the woods.

We were forty miles into the forest, seventy from the nearest town, one hundred and twenty from Tacoma. And it was like I could feel every mile of that distance. Could look around, could feel the air, and know how separate we were.

Kyle and I were fifteen. Kyle kept the car at about thirty-five, the Bug vibrating and shaking from the engine and from the pits and bumps in the road. The air poured in through the windows, swirling wet and cool across my arms, pushing lightly against my face. Rain from the night still covered the forest, the water seeming to spread the green. Green so dark it was black, green so bright it glowed.

I leaned my head and chest out the window, raising my body part-way into the wind and the passing leaves and I looked up at the thin band of blue sky above the road. Blue between the tops of trees moving slow and fast.

So blue.

Back in Tacoma, there were also cool, wet winds and branches and brush and green. But it wasn't at all the same.

We drove on a logging road somewhere in the valley of the Cispus and Cowlitz Rivers. Down to the southwest was Mount St. Helens, far up to the northeast was Mount Rainier. Kyle and I were at the Cispus camping for a few days.

I dropped from the window, falling back into my seat. Something wet and soft glanced off my shoulder. I raised my arm to block my face, grabbed a branch from near my feet and threw it at Kyle, hitting him in the ear, water and dirt splashing across his hair.

Kyle and I had been throwing branches and dirt and wood at each other for about fifteen minutes, picking the debris up from where it had gathered in the car over the past few days.

Kyle grabbed a branch and flung it at me, hitting me in the mouth, then threw a handful of leaves at me.

I gathered two handfuls of leaves and threw them at him. Kyle had been looking at the road and couldn't block them. They covered his face, rattling loudly in the wind.

"Bastard," I could hear him yelling. "Bastard."

Kyle threw a stick back at me and I had to close my eyes.

"Oh no," I heard Kyle say.

"What?" I said, looking, and now I saw a mud

puddle wider than the road and nine car lengths long. Tree bark bounced off my cheek. "Big puddle," I said.

Kyle yelled "Truce, Brian, truce" and I stopped myself from throwing the handful of dirt I was holding, Kyle pressing hard on the gas pedal and down-shifting to speed up the car. He was leaning forward, both hands on the wheel, staring at the puddle, his dark hair blowing from his face and eyes, the point of his jaw working steadily, teeth gnawing together. The engine was whining and I looked at Kyle and yelled, "No truce, no truce," as the car hit the puddle. I launched the dirt and two branches at him as the Bug slowed in a wave of brown water, the entire puddle seeming to pour over the hood, water spraying past the open windows, barely touching the insides of the doors. I threw a handful of small pebbles from my lap and now the front of the car was veering slightly to the left. The pebbles slapped against the windshield and Kyle's arm and face and the car was turning a little more, more, until now the wave was pouring through my window. The water covered my ear and neck and shoulder and I had to lean against Kyle to get away from it, steam spreading across the inside of the windshield and Kyle with one arm pushing me back toward my seat.

We reached the far shore of the puddle, the car shooting toward the left side of the road. Kyle was yelling, "Oh no oh no oh no," braking hard, the tires grinding loud as we slid across the dirt and rocks. We bumped head-on into a tree and I smacked my forehead against the windshield, fell back into the water on my seat.

Kyle was hitting his hand against the steering wheel and laughing without making any noise. I was laughing and holding onto the dashboard and door to keep myself above the water on my seat. Half an inch of it, brown, covered the metal floor. My arms were wet and my damp shirt clung to my side.

"Bastard," I said, still laughing. The engine had stopped and I could hear my voice echoing in the woods. "Why'd the water come through my window, not yours?" I said.

Kyle rocked in his seat, forward and back, his hair falling across his face, laughing. "Me," he said. "I planned that," he said, laughing harder now and more quietly. "I just didn't think it would work."

I was still holding myself in the air, clinging to the dashboard and door. I leaned against Kyle's head, pressing hard on it with my hand as I picked up a handful of leaves from the back seat, wiping off my face and then my seat.

"Oh my god," Kyle said, looking at me, the laughing starting again. "You're bleeding."

I put my hand to my forehead. Blood covered the ends of two fingers and Kyle laughed harder. I found a dry leaf and held it to my head, sitting back now in my seat.

Kyle was still laughing.

I leaned out the window to see if we had put a dent in the car. I could maybe see a small crease in the hood, but I wasn't sure if it hadn't already been there.

I heard Kyle drinking from a beer. I turned. He was looking out his window, staring at the bushes next to the car. He had stopped laughing, but apparently had no intention of leaving yet.

I found a bottle of beer in the back seat. The glass was cold against my lips and the beer was so cold it didn't have any taste.

I stared at the tree in front of us, holding the leaf to my head. The tree was extremely tall. Even leaning forward in my seat, I couldn't see its top through the windshield.

"So now," Kyle asked, his voice echoing quietly in the woods around us, "now do we go grouse hunting?"

"I think we are grouse hunting," I said. I took a drink.

A moment later, Kyle nodded. "True," he said. He leaned his head against the side of the door, staring up into the trees above us. "Grouse hunting has always been a very difficult and precise process," he said. "A small, wild, undomesticated cousin of the chicken, the grouse is very smart. It avoids all noise, almost never comes near the roads and, in most cases, ventures out only at dusk."

I drank again. Kyle drank again.

"That's why we hunt in a Volkswagen with a bad muffler," he said, "combing the logging roads in the middle of the day. Trick the enemy. Be smarter than him."

I nodded. I could hear the sound of my neck against my shirt collar as I moved. Could hear wind in the trees. Could hear water dripping from the sides of the car onto the damp ground below us.

"What is this place?" I asked. "I mean, who owns this land?"

Kyle's voice was distant. His whole head was out of his window now. He was looking at something above us. "I don't know," he said. "I'm sure it's not a park," he said, "and I'm fairly sure it's okay for us to camp around here."

I heard a clicking sound outside. A bird, I thought. Kyle maybe.

"The state?" Kyle asked, voice still far away. "Maybe they own it. Or the feds."

I drank again, the beer now tasting like something more than cold. I pressed back in my seat, raising my feet to press them against the dashboard. I was still holding the leaf to my head. I moved it now, finding another dry spot and pressing again at the cut.

In a moment, I heard Kyle say, "Probably a logging company."

"Yes," I said. Nodding. Turning to look at him and hearing my voice in the woods. "Probably a logging company."

I saw a pint of bourbon in the water at my feet. We'd been drinking from it the night before. I opened the wet bottle and swallowed, the whiskey warm and like smoke in my mouth and then very smoky, very warm and burning in my throat and chest.

I took a drink of my beer, holding the wet bottle of bourbon out to Kyle. It was a moment and he looked my way, saw the bottle, me. He took a drink.

After another minute, he looked out the back window, then out the front windshield. "Right," he said.

The engine started, loud, and I moved the leaf, trying to find a new dry spot to press against my head.

Kyle slid the gearshift into reverse and backed us away from the tree. He put the car in first gear and we started forward.

"We're moving," I said.

"I've decided we're not quite there yet," Kyle said.

I nodded. The car was moving faster now, the trees again forming a blurring tunnel around us. "Not quite where?" I asked.

Kyle's voice drifted in the wind now moving through the car again. I heard him say, "We haven't found grouse country."

A small white tree was bent across the road. The Bug passed under it, branches scraping against the hood and windshield and then the thin trunk hitting the roof. The car was up to speed, shaking and bouncing again. The road turned and the trees were low and stood away from us, the corridor of forest opening. Far ahead, I saw the dense green of a tall hill of fir trees, the slope leading down to the lake nearby.

The road turned, the walls forming around us again.

"Grouse country is not a particular place," I said, voice half lost to the sound of the driving car.

"It's an uncommon mix of field and bushes and trees. There's got to be a feeling in the trees and bushes." I took a drink. "It's in the place and what you see in the place."

Kyle was nodding and down-shifting, thin body leaning forward, just slightly hunched over. He looked at me, eyes colorless in the shadows of the forest. "That's pretty good," he said.

I leaned toward the open window and took a drink from the new beer, dropping the leaf now and seeing it fall toward my lap, then catch in the air, swirling once with the wind and then out the window and gone. The wind hit my face and twisted my hair, the beer heavy against my teeth, and I swallowed again and the drink was pushing farther through my mouth and neck, swallowed again and the heaviness spread and filled my chest.

We climbed along the river's ridge. Through the trees on my side I saw the Cowlitz a hundred yards below, the water blue and flowing and in some places shimmering with the sunlight. Across the river I saw three deer along the bank, standing. Above us in the band of blue, the sun was bright and through the branches and tree tops it laid patches of yellow on the road and reflected in flashes off the wet hood. The flashes were bright and warm on my face, seeming to fill my mouth and nose and eyes.

"Someday we should drive to Alaska," I heard Kyle say. "Get work on a boat. Drive back before winter."

I nodded. It seemed very far away. I remembered I was with Kyle. I said, "It seems very far away."

He turned to me, light flashing across his face as it broke through the leaves and branches. He smiled some, turned back to the road.

I took a drink and a drop of beer fell from the edge of the bottle onto the door. The drop slid toward the arm rest, riding along the water still covering the door, disappearing before it reached the handle.

"Not so far," I heard Kyle say. "A couple days."

"Being eighteen," I said. "Leaving. That's what seems far away."

He nodded, drinking from his beer, the other hand barely touching the wheel and the light now moving so fast, not rushed, just fast as it slid across the windshield, through the car, over both of us.

He turned to me and smiled again. "Not so far," he said.

My hand was out the window and it caught a wet, whole leaf, feeling smooth and cool in my fingers. I held it, drinking from the whiskey, the label soft and wet and sliding across the glass, smoky and burning on my tongue. Bright light on the windshield, and in the sudden bursts I saw dust in the air and the reflection of my face in the glass.

"Okay," I said quietly. "Okay."

"Not so far," he said.

And I drank again, among the flashes, sudden light so close, the dust on the glass, the trees and road ahead and my face, my face there that I hadn't seen in days, that I felt warm light against, light holding my jaw, pressing on my eyes, seeing the river to the side still bright and my hand out the window in the leaves, the road ahead and beside and behind, all moving slow then fast then a blur.

2 TACOMA

I can remember riding along Pacific Avenue in downtown Tacoma, coming back from the mall with Will Wilson's parents. Will Wilson's step-dad was laughing as he drove, pointing at the prostitutes, all of them in high heels and tight jeans or skirts, hanging out along the small strip of adult video stores and pawn shops and bars across from the bus station.

Will Wilson's mom didn't look up, just read some magazine in her lap. Mr. Wilson was looking in his rearview mirror, saying to Will Wilson and me in the back seat, "When you're old like me, you can get some of that, young men." And then he said to Jodi, his niece sitting next to me who lived with them off and on through high school, "If you're not careful, little girl, you'll end up here with these fine women."

Will Wilson and I were thirteen years old. Jodi was eleven.

The car had stopped at a light and Mr. Wilson was staring over at a couple of groups of women. "Young men, they're not as bad as they look," he said, reaching to shake his wife's magazine. "Don't I know, honey."

In the back seat were the dirty magazines, the ones that Will Wilson and me would look at in the bathroom at his house. Pictures of naked women and men, naked girls and boys. Pictures I always thought about later, that made my knees and thighs ache. Made my teeth hurt some. Pictures that I would only stare at, wondering where these people lived, if they worked in jobs, if they went to school. Wondering if the things they did felt good to them. Wondering if they liked any of it at all.

And that day the car sat at a stop light, the light turning green and red again without us moving, Mrs. Wilson never looking up as Mr. Wilson asked her if she wanted to play hooker and the pimp that night, asked her if she wanted to pick up some nigger whore and play monkey and the zoo keepers, or masters and the slave. And Will Wilson and I were in the back seat barely listening, looking at the pictures. Jodi looking over my shoulder at the magazine, not talking loudly like she usually did.

Jodi had a wide, somehow square face, was wearing red jeans and a blue shirt. She was a cute tomboy who, even though she was just five feet and maybe a hundred pounds, could always keep up with the rest of us, whether we were running through the gulch or drinking beer.

In the car, Will Wilson and I had pushed Jodi away so she couldn't see the pictures. And then Jodi did start talking loud, telling jokes about Mr. and Mrs. Wilson, dumb jokes that didn't have punch lines and were about them making bad dinners or not flushing the toilet.

Mr. Wilson was saying for her to stop. But Jodi

kept talking.

"Jodi, god damn it," Mr. Wilson yelled, "that's it, put your head down here, put it here between the seats." He had long hair and a mustache and was drinking a beer that he kept between his legs. His hard face had turned red and he was watching Jodi in the rearview mirror. "God damn it," he was yelling, "put it down here."

The car still hadn't moved.

Jodi did put her head in the space between the front bucket seats and Mr. Wilson flicked her in the head any time she made a motion. But even though she'd put her head down without a fight, she kept opening her mouth like she was going to speak and "I told you!" he'd yell and then flick, he'd snap her in the head with his finger. That finger hurt too, because although he was not a big guy, he was a guy who flicked her hard and flicked Will Wilson hard and me too, if I was at the house screwing around with Will Wilson and we woke up Mr. Wilson while he was sleeping before night shift, then he would flick me in the head.

And so at one o'clock on that Sunday afternoon when we were driving back from the mall, I was watching Mr. Wilson with his thin body all pulled up, sitting forward in the driver's seat, car stopped at a light that had now turned green twice. Mr. Wilson was watching Jodi. Hand raised. Waiting.

Flick.

And finally he had to give up. Jodi kept talking. Mr. Wilson sat back and the light turned green again, but the car didn't move. He looked over at the hookers, smiling. He said, "Women are so fucking fuckable, that's the thing. Isn't it honey? Especially the pros like that. But all of them. So wonderfully fuckable. So good at that."

Jodi sat up and started to tell a knock-knock joke, giving both the question and answer.

"Knock-knock. Who's there? Mr. Wilson. Mr. Wilson Who?"

And Mr. Wilson turned fast, in one motion punching Jodi hard across the face. Will Wilson glancing up from his magazine. In a moment turning back.

•

The two sets of tracks stretched forward as far as the flashlight would reach, dying in the blackness of the tunnel's slow curve to the left. The five of us were about a half mile into the train tunnel that led from the smelter to the Narrows Bridge. Will Wilson and Coe, Teddy and me, and this cool, quiet kid named Clarence Stark.

Every few minutes, Will Wilson had been turning off the light. The first times the tunnel's pure darkness echoed with our moaning, screaming laughs. But now, twenty minutes into the tunnel, Will Wilson turned the light off and we all were silent except for the sharp gravel crunching under our feet, the sound of us sucking dank air into our lungs. All of us waiting for someone to give in and laugh or scream.

Will Wilson had brought Stark out with us that night, something Will Wilson had never done before. This was early spring when we were sixteen and even though the four of us usually talked to other kids at parties and the waterfront, few of them got in the car with us and none of them had ever gone down into the gulch with us.

Stark was a thin kid with a crew cut head and these dark, almost black eyes. He was always smiling slightly, nodding a little. I knew him from a couple of classes. Although, when he came to my house with Will Wilson that night, Stark and I just nodded to each other and it was like we were meeting for the first time.

The five of us had stolen a big Delta 88 earlier that night, Will Wilson driving us in it across town, finally taking us to a small bridge I'd never been on near the abandoned copper smelter. Sixty feet below, in a narrow, man-made valley that cut through an offshoot of the gulch, was the entrance to a train tunnel.

And as we'd first walked into it, Will Wilson was telling Stark about parties the four of us had had, about other cars we'd stolen. And he said something about girls, saying how later that night we would find some, making it sound like the girls were just waiting for us.

Will Wilson was trying to sell us to Stark. Will Wilson was trying to bring him in.

Now, nearly a half mile inside the tunnel, long after it had begun a gradual turn, we all walked in the dark, waiting for someone to laugh or yell. And then a bottle exploded above us, someone having finally broken the silence. The flashlight came on, seeming to bounce around, shining on the walls, then the arched ceiling, then the ground, Will Wilson aiming the light at each of us, holding his face, cheek bleeding between his fingers. The light stopping on Coe, who'd thrown the bottle, as Will Wilson pulled a shard of glass from his face.

Will Wilson had hit Coe four times in the side of his head with his open hand before Coe could drop to his knees and hold his arms over his head and start saying, "Oh fuck, man. I'm sorry, man."

Stark was across from me in the dim light, staring at Will Wilson. Not blinking. Not moving. But leaning back just slightly. Leaning away.

Will Wilson kept swinging at Coe's head.

And I felt it across my hands then. I turned and saw Teddy staring forward into the bend in the tunnel. Saw his hair blowing. Felt the breeze pushing across my face.

I glanced back at Will Wilson, saw his hand in a fist now as he waited for Coe to uncover himself, Coe's arms smeared with Will Wilson's blood, moving fast as he tried to cover his whole head. But Stark stepped up to Will Wilson and touched him on the shoulder, something I would never have done. Will Wilson turned on Stark, face tight, hand still in a fist. Then he looked down the tunnel.

The breeze was now like a light wind.

"Oh golly," Will Wilson said, smiling some, hand releasing. Stepping forward to stand ahead of us. "Golly, golly, golly."

A light appeared on the right side of the tunnel. The headlight shine of an unseen train.

"We can run back," Coe said, eyes wide and looking into the wind. "It's not so far."

"Stand up, Coe," I said. "Don't run. Don't be stupid."

"Listen to Porter," Will Wilson said. "Listen to the voice of reason."

I glanced at the wall. "Will," I said evenly, "shine the light on the wall. Near the track."

He looked at me, smiling. Blood still dripping down his cheek. "Why?"

"Shine the light on the track near the wall," I said quietly.

He did. And all of us except Coe could see the problem.

"What?" Coe was asking loudly, standing, the oily dirt and gravel stuck to his jeans. "What?"

When we'd first walked into the tunnel, there'd been about six feet between each of the outside rails and the wall. Enough space that you could, if you had to, stand up against the wall to let a train pass. But without our noticing, the space had disappeared. The tunnel had narrowed. A train would nearly touch the tunnel wall when it passed. And so, before the train came, we'd have to be sure we moved to the opposite side of the tunnel.

"Make the right choice," Will Wilson said.

"What?" Coe screamed. "What?"

"How about if another train comes?" Teddy was asking me, his voice straining to yell from behind me, coming only quietly in the wind.

"I think that you get on the ground," I said to Teddy, just barely aiming my voice over my shoulder, thinking I should turn to him, help him, but I was still staring at the growing light. "The gravel in the middle of the two sets of tracks," I told him. "Lay down there."

Teddy had been my neighbor friend when we were kids. He lived with his mom and dad next door. He was a really nice kid who I'd played with when there was nothing else to do. There was something just so nice about Teddy. Something about him that wanted to do good.

The light was bright across the right wall, the wind ripping so strong across my ears that I could barely hear Coe still screaming, "What? What?"

Then there was the whistle. Teddy lowered his head. Coe stopped yelling. And I glanced at Stark, saw him staring straight ahead, crouched slightly, leaning back from the light and wind and noise.

And I remember wondering how Will Wilson could have made this turn out so good for Stark.

The white headlight appeared and the engine of a train was coming around the corner, tilted, turning, growing from nothing, from the bend in the tunnel. There was the sound of steel and wheels on the track and the diesel engine roaring loud. A train coming at us. One hundred and fifty feet away.

Except that with the engine tilted, the light shining in our faces, it was hard to see which track the train was on.

"Which track?" I was yelling and Will Wilson was shaking his head, smiling.

I could see the other cars as the whistle blew again, eliminating the sound of the wind and the engine and our voices.

Maybe seventy feet away. Fifty.

"Left track," I yelled and moved right. "It's on the left track."

Teddy and Coe followed me, hands pressing against the right wall. But Will Wilson and Stark didn't hear me and couldn't see for themselves. They dropped to the ground between the two sets of tracks, the train now passing, all wind and high grinding engine and whistle blowing and all that crash of noise shaking through my chest and ears and face. Ten feet from me. Just a few feet from Will Wilson and Stark.

And after the train had passed, Will Wilson smiled some and said that Teddy and Coe and me hadn't really felt it on the other side of the tunnel.

And with Will Wilson saying how the wind had been right there next to him, how the engine and wheels had been just a few feet away, with Stark nodding slightly, smiling beside Will Wilson, I did start to feel like I'd missed out on something good.

We were out of the tunnel, walking along the tracks toward the Narrows Bridge, half a mile away. It was a tall, green suspension bridge, a mile across, a few hundred feet above the water. Two steel towers rose up from the Narrows Straight, each standing five hundred feet high. Heavy, pipe-like cables stretched from land to the towers in half arcs, in the center the cables forming wide, pure arcs as they swept down from both towers to the slightly bowed road.

The five of us were ten feet from the wide Narrows Straight, the water near the beach lapping quietly on the rocks. A steep hill was to our left, the trees and leaves wet and thick. I could see the few scattered lights on the far side of the straight, could see car headlights crossing over the bridge. But we were alone. Seeming to have passed through that tunnel into a place so far from anything. Miles from our houses, just following these tracks.

Behind us, a mile away, there was a flashing light at the top of the smokestack at the abandoned copper smelter. Once, when my dad had been a little drunk and happy, he'd talked about being a boy. He and his brothers had been outside and suddenly they smelled chlorine. Back then, bitter, sick clouds of it would blow unseen through Tacoma when the copper smelter's tall smokestack was being cleaned. My dad and his brothers would smell the chlorine and run down the block gagging and covering their mouths and when they'd run into their house their mother would be there getting ready to leave for work and she'd say, "That's the chlorine from the smelter cleaners. That means your dad is up there, right now, scrubbing the stack."

My dad never spoke to his dad. They lived just three miles apart, though, and I would sometimes see my dad's dad at the store buying beer. I'd stare at him as I waited in line, standing behind him with my half rack and fake i.d., thinking of him as a stranger who looked a lot like me.

But, walking now, I turned away from the smelter. I didn't want to think about my dad or his dad.

Teddy and Coe were trying to walk on the rails with their eyes closed. "It's like practice for the D.W.I. tests," Coe said. "Walk this line. Touch your nose."

Every few steps, Coe's heavy feet slipped off the rail.

Stark was walking next to me. "I'd have jumped to the side too," Stark said quietly. "Except I couldn't move. Basically, I fell down."

We both laughed some without making noise, both facing away from Will Wilson.

But already I knew I shouldn't be laughing. Knew you couldn't hide something from Will Wilson. I turned toward Will Wilson now. "What are we doing?" I asked loudly. "Will? Where are we going?"

"I was thinking," Will Wilson said, "about those towers."

We were all quiet, walking forward along the tracks, looking up toward the big red and white steel towers that held the ends of the power lines stretching across the Narrows.

"About climbing them," he said.

And it was a moment before Coe started to run. And we all ran after him. Racing toward the electrical towers.

Clarence Stark could run very fast. He'd already caught Coe, then Will Wilson, then he was running in the lead. I could see the two towers above us on the hill, thick steel and four main legs, a crosshatched pattern of small and large steel beams. Both towers a few hundred feet high, surrounded by chain-link fences. I was still running when I saw Stark hit the chain-link fence around one of the towers, saw him climbing the fourteen feet to the coils of barbed wire, Will Wilson climbing below him, Coe stopping at the bottom and breathing hard. Teddy and I were headed toward the other tower, the toes of my shoes finding footing as I smacked into the metal fence, my climbing slowed some as I grabbed the top wire between barbs, lifting myself over and catching the mesh again.

Stark was climbing a ladder that led to the top of his tower, Will Wilson twenty feet below him. And I was breathing hard, smiling as I ran to the ladder on our tower, finding the steps and starting to climb.

Teddy and I were only halfway up by the time Stark and Will Wilson had reached the top of the other tower, the two of them already walking around a small platform just below the terminals, the cables sloping down over the Narrows, up again to the other side.

I could see more of the water and the bridge as I climbed. Could see the lights of a few scattered homes farther down the Narrows Straight. I looked over my shoulder toward the tunnel we'd come from, could see the smelter stack as a black column against the dark night sky. I climbed and the air was much colder and I saw how this hill along

the tracks was a part of the gulch, how it reached
through a park and a neighborhood to the waterfront, and I climbed thinking that I might even see
beyond the smelter to the lights of the Tide Flats
and even Browns Point, and I looked at the Narrows Bridge and felt myself so high in the air, and I
climbed, not thinking about the car we'd stolen or
the fight we'd had or what we might do as the night
went on, only pulling myself up, looking around,
going higher, pulling faster, exhaling white, my
fingers numb, seeing in the sky more of the reflection of the lights of Tacoma, thinking only that soon
I'd even be able to see past the smelter, that I'd see
the houses and streets and cars of most, even all, of
the North End where I'd always lived and where
then climbing I knew, suddenly, without meaning
to think it, without even wanting it, I knew I'd find
some way to leave, and I wondered for a second
what Kyle was doing right then.

And I looked toward Stark and Will Wilson,
at the top of their tower, less than a hundred feet
away, their smiling faces lit pale white from arcs
of electricity. Blue-white arcs that reached from the
cable terminals to their hands. They were smiling
and I slowed my climbing and I could hear one
of them happily yelling, "Hey. Hey." Their arms
raised, both of them stepping from side to side, hair
standing up from their heads, the arcs bending and
stretching, lighting so white their smiles.

And then one arc ground out and there was
a flash of white and I thought I saw flames, but he
was already turned black and killed. Clarence Stark

was dead.

And Teddy was below me saying, "It's great, Brian. I can see everything, Brian. Brian, it's great."

I was the one to go for help, running along the train tracks to the base of the bridge, then climbing up a dirt hill to the lovers lane park there. On a pay phone I told the police what had happened and where I was and I expected all of them to show up at this park, have to carry their gear down the path to the waterfront. But only one police car pulled up to me, then took me down a service road the five of us hadn't seen, a road the ambulance and fire trucks had already gone down.

And beyond my still remembering the image of Will Wilson smiling sickly, stepping backward as Stark collapsed at his feet, remembering hanging onto my ladder three quarters of the way up as the burnt smell blew past me, beyond all that there was an angry disappointment I couldn't stop – an embarrassment that we hadn't been so isolated, that we'd been near a service road all along.

The story was in the paper the next day. A story about the death of a promising young high school student named Clarence Stark. It mentioned the names of the four survivors, Michael Coe, Brian Porter, Theodore Selva and William Wilson. I'd never been in the paper. I cut out the article. I stared at our names. They seemed bigger than the other words. They seemed formal and important.

Some teachers and students blamed us for Stark's death. Although no one ever said that to us. They just glanced at one of us if Clarence Stark was mentioned, sometimes stopping short, staring for a moment before they said his name.

In the days after Stark died, Will Wilson and Coe got beaten by their parents. Black eyes. Bruised arms.

Teddy was put on restriction for two weeks, though he was out with us again in one.

My dad stared as I told him the story. Then he stood and leaned forward, touching my shoulder, leaving for work, but saying he was sorry that kid died. Saying, "Be careful, Brian. Be careful."

We would meet more people in the next few years of high school, would go to all the parties we could find, hang out in the waterfront parking lots with everyone else. But we never invited someone else along on anything we did. More and more the four of us seemed to be coming from something else, heading off to do something more. And people knew it.

The night below the power towers, as the four of us sat in a row on the edge of an ambulance's steel bumper, the police charged us with possession of alcohol and trespassing on state property. Teddy was quiet and almost shaking. Coe and me nodded. But Will Wilson was still smiling sickly, still just staring.

And I think he knew, even then. I think he knew. Knew, exactly, what it meant.

There'd been death in our lives.

A few months after the accident, I can remember being in Will Wilson's car with two girls, both of them quietly asking about Clarence Stark, quietly asking if I'd seen him die. And I smiled just slightly, and so did Will Wilson, leaning toward them, touching, and in a moment both of us said yes.

•

"Show him," Coe had said to her. Amelia was sitting on the couch, staring at the TV. "Show him," Coe said again.

Will Wilson was laughing. He took a bite from his pear. He chewed and the fruit was white and wet in his half-open mouth. He said, "She's not just going to show me."

My dad paid to have a baby-sitter for me in the summers till I was eleven, which is surprising in a way. But when I was a little kid, a neighborhood girl would be at my house after school and on the nights my dad was out drinking or working graveyard shift. The baby-sitters cleaned some and cooked dinner. Tomato soup and toast, macaroni and cheese. When I was ten and eleven years old, my baby-sitter was a junior high girl named Amelia. She had long black hair and was taller than me. She wore white t-shirts and bell bottom jeans, sneakers or clogs.

Teddy would come over to my house most every day and he and Amelia and me would play Wiffle bat baseball in the front yard, using the old three-fifty engine on blocks near the street as home plate and then hitting the plastic ball toward the house. The roof was a home run, the windows a triple, the concrete steps of the porch a double. It was a small yard and we hit a lot of home runs. We would set the stereo speakers in the front door and listen to Amelia's cassette tapes of Elton John and the Bee Gees.

Kyle came over once, early that summer when I was eleven and we played baseball with Teddy and Amelia. Kyle was usually gone a lot in the summers, working on fishing boats owned by his uncles. Teddy liked Kyle a lot, from school, and always asked if he'd be coming over. Even when we were older, Teddy would still talk to me about playing baseball with Kyle in the summer, as if we'd done it all the time, which we hadn't.

Most summer days, after Teddy left and before my dad came home, Amelia would sit with me at the kitchen table and read a book to me. I could read then, I was ten or eleven, but I liked that she would read to me.

I thought Amelia was very pretty.

I'd met Michael Coe just that year. He was the heavy kid with stringy hair who would watch Kyle and me build dams in the rain at recess and who'd I sat next to in fifth grade. Michael and his friend Will Wilson had started coming over to my house after school.

"What are you going to do?" Will Wilson asked, face so smoothly tight as he smiled, eyes still staring at me without blinking.

I looked at Teddy, saw him watching the TV very closely. Coe walked quickly toward Amelia, as if he could surprise her. She didn't move. He reached for her arm. She pulled away easily.

"Get away from me," she said quietly.

Coe got a hold of her arm again and it took her a moment to shake off his thick hand.

"Turn off the TV," Will Wilson said. Coe turned the volume down and then off. Teddy still stared at the dark screen. Amelia stared for a moment, then swung her head around, looking at Will Wilson and Coe standing and me sitting on the floor near Teddy, and I could see that she'd started grinding her front teeth.

"Really," she said. "No."

Coe grabbed her arm and she shook it off. She moved very little, though. As if by sitting still, this all would pass her by.

Coe and Will Wilson said they liked coming over to my house because I didn't have a mom and so no one would watch us. We dug big holes in the backyard and buried my trucks and GI Joes.

Sometimes the four of us would make houses out of cardboard boxes and stuff them with newspaper and light them on fire on the small, unfinished patio in the backyard. Amelia would stand in the doorway and say, "If you burn the house down, Brian. Don't burn the house down, Brian." The flames would pour through the cutout cardboard windows and doors, sometimes curling high toward the branches of the neighbor's pear tree. Then the four of us, Will Wilson, Coe, Teddy and me, all grabbed for the garden hose and usually Will Wilson ended up with it and he would point the nozzle away from the fire, saying, "Wait. One second. Wait. A second more. Let it burn."

"Get the arm, Teddy," Will Wilson said and Teddy didn't move. "Damn it, Teddy," Will Wilson said. "Listen to me. Do something. Get the arm."

Teddy stood and walked slowly across the room. He carefully grabbed Amelia's forearm, held it away from him, looking at it. Amelia started to move and he dropped the arm.

"You idiot," Will Wilson said.

Late that summer, the four of us and Amelia had started having very big water fights at my house, with buckets and hoses and balloons and slingshots to shoot the balloons.

One time Will Wilson took two balloons and chased Amelia across the backyard to the front and down the street and she was very fast and he couldn't catch her. Amelia came back a few minutes later, smiling and waving at Will Wilson. And when the game had ended and everyone was wet and no one was chasing anyone anymore, Will Wilson quietly followed Amelia inside the house. He was carrying two balloons again and he snuck up behind her, she said later, telling me she didn't even hear him open the bedroom door, didn't notice him till he touched her shoulders and reached past her neck and dropped two balloons down her shirt. He squeezed her hard with both his arms till the balloons broke. She turned and he stood staring, she said. Not smiling. Just standing so still. And then he walked out of the room.

"Really," Amelia said evenly and with her free arm she hit once at Coe. "Come on."

Coe grabbed the arm again and she stopped mov-

ing. Teddy stood watching him.

Will Wilson looked at me and he was smiling the way he did then, the way he would through junior high and high school, smiling with his teeth showing and the tip of his tongue showing, the pink tip rubbing his lower lip. And he stared at me and said, "Well?" and I stood and grabbed Amelia's foot and I didn't look at her face.

"No, Brian," she said. "Stop this."

Coe and I couldn't keep her still. She hit Coe in the shoulder and kept getting the arm free from him.

I couldn't get myself to hold her leg very tightly.

"No," she said louder and dragged out the word and Amelia had started kicking now and swinging harder because Will Wilson was behind me and then past me and he had dropped the pear core on the carpet, was holding both of her arms above her head and now she couldn't move.

The four of us would play poker at my house, using peanuts to bet and playing games Will Wilson's step-dad had taught him. Will Wilson would turn the radio to one of the Seattle rock stations so we could listen to Led Zeppelin and The Who and Black Sabbath. Amelia would sometimes sit at the green kitchen table with us and play too and after a few minutes Will Wilson would smile and say, "So, let's play strip poker."

And Amelia would say, "Forget about it little Willie."

Will Wilson was taller than the rest of us and only a couple inches shorter than Amelia, but he was skinny, kind of bony, and Amelia liked to call him little Willie.

"On the floor," Will Wilson said.

We slid her onto the carpet. Will Wilson was kneeling behind her, holding her arms. I was holding a knee and Coe was across from me holding the other one and that way we kept the feet from kicking us. We were looking back at Will Wilson across her body. Waiting.

Teddy was standing behind Coe. I was trying not to look at him.

"Shit," I could hear Amelia say, the back of her head pressed against Will Wilson's thighs. "No."

Will Wilson said, "Pull her shirt up."

Coe pulled the shirt up and there was a small, white bra and Will Wilson quickly took the shirt over her head and arms without Amelia getting loose.

Teddy said slowly, "I thought you were just pantsing her."

Will Wilson said quietly, "Teddy, get on the fucking floor with us. You are standing there like a dumbshit."

Amelia's head fell back against Will Wilson's thighs, then jerked forward, straining to get away, only hovering above his jeans.

On the other side of Will Wilson's alley that summer, there was a high school girl who would lay out in the sun on a towel. The four of us would crouch in the gravel, hiding behind the dented trash cans lining the fence. This older girl wore a pink bikini and we would stare at her through the slats of wood.

One time Will Wilson whispered over his shoulder to the rest of us, "We should pants her someday."

"What's that?" Teddy asked me quietly. His face was close to mine and his eyebrows were low and worried.

I shook my head, but didn't say anything. I didn't want Will Wilson to hear that I didn't know.

Will Wilson said, "You run up behind her and yank her jeans down. So you can see her underpants. But I bet this one doesn't wear them."

"Why doesn't she wear underwear?" I asked.

Will Wilson said, "My step-dad says she's the neighborhood slut."

"What's a slut?" Teddy asked me.

I shook my head, but didn't say anything.

Will Wilson whispered over his shoulder, "It's like a prostitute who doesn't charge."

Will Wilson had his hand under Amelia's back and he was struggling some. "Fuck," he said. "Fuck."

"Damn it, William. Brian. Brian. Stop him."

And then Will Wilson smiled. The bra came loose and he pulled it over her arms without her getting away. Pale skin and red nipples. Small, smooth breasts.

"No," she said. "Really."

The room was quiet and she was struggling and Coe and I held her tightly now. Only her hips could move. Teddy was across from me on his knees next to Coe. And then Will Wilson looked at us three kids crowded close around him over Amelia. And he smiled.

"It's like wrestling," Will Wilson said to the three of us at school that day. "You try to get her pants down. It's like a game. They like it."

Teddy asked, "Have you done this before?"

"No, but fuck," Will Wilson said. "Amelia's

always playing around with us."

"I don't think she'll like it," I said.

"So you're not going to do it," he said.

"No."

"So you're going to say we shouldn't come over."

"No."

"So you're worried your dad will find out and you might get in trouble."

"No."

"So what then?"

"Get the pants," Will Wilson said and Coe unzipped Amelia's jeans.

"Stop it," she said loudly and it was almost like she was yelling and that scared me. "Damn it, Brian. No."

But Coe was pulling down the jeans and there were pink underwear with flowers on them. "Keep the knees together," Will Wilson said and I pushed the knee toward Coe and I was for a second close to him, his slick hair and wet mouth. Coe nodded at me as he pulled the jeans under our hands and then I felt how the knee was kind of cold and the skin around it rough and I was looking at her legs jerking and the white white skin of her thighs, my face feeling numb and heavy.

Teddy was absently folding Amelia's jeans. He'd only touched her once.

Amelia jerked her knee and my hand fell, touched her smooth belly and the edge of her almost slippery pink panties.

"Don't touch her there," Will Wilson said to me. "Fuck, Porter. Then it's like rape."

And I pulled my hand away fast, scared by what

Will Wilson had said, sure that I'd almost done something very wrong. And I was careful now just to touch her enough to keep her in place, holding her down as the four of us all stared, looking at her and not talking for a minute, not talking or laughing, only watching that body, seeing it strain against our hands, seeing the bare knees and belly, the small thighs, the breasts. Will Wilson finally letting go of her hands, the rest of us pulling away too, and we watched her run to the bathroom with her clothes.

•

When we were seventeen and eighteen, we'd wake up at Wilson's cousin's house. It was a house on an empty road between two neighborhoods, some unplanned mid point between subdivisions. It was like a lot of places I remember in Tacoma, one of those forgotten roads lined by high fences and tall overgrown bushes and lit just barely by intermittent streetlights. Sometimes there'd be a store, a corner store with faded advertisements for cigarette deals and inexpensive beer, and in a few places there'd be duplexes or old storefronts, doors that faced these forgotten roads, dark doorways that looked abandoned, until you looked close and you saw something, mail in the mail box or the flickering blue light of a TV behind a curtain or a tricycle pressed against the side of the building, and you realized that someone was home.

That's the kind of place where Will Wilson lived and where his cousin lived and it was the kind of street we all four lived on.

It was always damp in his cousin's house and smelled bad and you'd wake up on the thin hard carpet feeling sick and feeling like you'd never slept at all. His cousin was always teaching himself to play the guitar, this bright pink guitar he'd bought at a pawn shop and that he'd rigged up to run through the old console stereo that just about filled one wall of the living room, which was one of only a few rooms in that whole house, so a lot of the time I'd end up sleeping against that hard wooden stereo with the tan cloth over the speakers. I'd wake up hearing the feedback still ringing quietly from the speakers, my face against the floor and having to pee, feeling cold and wet in my jacket, wet maybe from the night before out in the rain or just wet from the air in the house, with the curtains pulled shut and the floor and couch almost damp when you touched them. I'd wake up in the silence, turning over and staring up at that gray ceiling sprayed rough with texture and mixed with the thousand glimmering bits of pink and green and gold, laying there feeling so gray through my body, hurting, and wanting to throw up, and staring up at that ceiling and hearing the buzz from the speakers next to me and hearing the others sleeping in the room and remembering all that beer we'd drank and the half gallon of gin and the dope his cousin's friend had had, because you couldn't not remember it, every drink and all that smoke now so deep in every part of your body, turned sick now and dying, and for me staring at that ceiling glimmering pink and green, I could remember every drink and every breath of smoke and I would feel it still, wondering now if I was really sick or just stoned or drunk, all of it turning bad through the end of the night, the drinking and smoking that had finally just sunk you, so you'd only known to drink more, drinking through the smoking hoping another drink would make you feel like you had when you'd started, that soft warm moment of the first hit of the pot and the first sip of the first beer and the first scent of gin when one of the others opened a bottle. But now it was lost, everything awful, and worn, and gone. And I'd sit up finally, here in this house among my sleeping friends, finding Will Wilson sitting up, on the couch, sipping a beer, staring at me, gray eyes in a leathered face, nodding at me like he'd never gone to sleep.

Bad things had happened. I'd feel my hand then and know we'd gone out and fought. Know we'd driven to each corner of Tacoma. Know we'd found girls. I'd close my eyes and see dark figures tearing at each other, hidden faces in the black backyards of the houses we'd passed, faces turning gray as they ran in groups through the pale white light of empty parking lots.

And I'd blink my eyes and know there'd been a dream I'd just woken up from, on the floor, that I couldn't quite remember, a dream of the hidden faces in groups, in backyards, roaming.

Bad things had happened. We'd started here and ended up here, in the quiet of this small, forgotten, almost unidentifiable home near the gulch.

"What happened?" I'd ask Will Wilson then, my mouth hurting just to speak.

And he'd sip beer. "Fuck you," he'd say, swallowing. "You know. You know what happened."

"Hung over," I'd say, and close my eyes, touch them lightly with one hand, then another, pain shooting through my eyes to the top of my head, my neck, the front of my chest.

"Fuck you," he'd say. "You were right there."

And I'd still have my eyes in my hands, pressing just that bit harder, the pain going white, with the other hand finding a valium in the pocket of my jeans, slipping it across my lips, biting it once before swallowing it down.

And I'd be nodding now. Saying, "Right," realizing my face was damp too, like the carpet and my jacket and the insides of my jeans, and I'd know that I was damp from this house we were in and from the rain we'd run through and from the sweat of all that we'd done. "Yes," I'd say. "Yes, you're right."

2   DRIVING AWAY

I'm bouncing lightly against the trunk, elbows pressed against the green, heavy steel. I can feel the metal springing in and out, making a quiet sound that's part gong, part hillbilly saw.

Table Rock, Wyoming. Two days and eight hundred miles into the drive. We are planning to stop for the night soon.

Kyle stands on the other side of the car, leaning against the gas pump. The station's corrugated metal roof rattles above us as the wind grows stronger, going silent as the gusts diminish. The wind is blowing across what looks like farmland here, pushing warm and solid against my face.

The tall, thin attendant stands near the station door, staring toward the fields.

"What's the worst name you can imagine for yourself?" Kyle asks. He's squinting as he stares out at the farmland.

The quiet bell of the gas pump rings every few seconds, the price numbers rolling with a slow, constant whir and periodic click.

"For me," Kyle says, "there is always Alex."

I'm glad we aren't talking about anything but this. Glad we're not talking about me smelling like smoke. Or about how that could have happened. I'm glad I'm with Kyle. I know that I have missed him.

"Alex," I repeat slowly.

"I'd be less capable than I'd want to be," he says. "Less capable than an Alex thinks he should be."

I nod my head, looking more in the direction of the trunk than Kyle.

The gas pump whirs.

I exhale slowly, the breath a kind of emptying stretch. My own release. Forgetting the huts, forgetting Tacoma. I look at Kyle, his shifting, vaporous reflection in the car.

"Roger," I say, staring absently at my blurry face in the trunk, strands of my long hair falling forward. "That'd be my name."

"A skinny kid," Kyle says. "Skinny as sticks," he says and smiles. "They'd call you Sticks."

"As a child I'd be afraid of going to the circus," I say.

Kyle frowns, green eyes almost disappearing. In a moment, the frown ends. He says quietly, "You told me you really were afraid of the circus."

I nod. "I still am."

"Roger is, or Brian?"

I nod again. "Me," I say.

Eight gallons. The wind blows hair off my face. The gas man shifts his weight to his other foot, his hips swinging in a quick little jig.

"Roger," I say. I begin to bounce lightly against the trunk again. My dim reflection bending then shrinking. In a moment, I say, "Afraid of the circus."

"But you don't know why," Kyle says.

"You're right," I say. "I don't know why."

"It's because they seem to know something you don't," Kyle says. "Because they are hidden behind make up and costumes," he says. "Because they come off the stage and enter the crowd and leave town the next day without ever giving their names," he says.

And he smiles, and nods, and his reflection disappears, reappears, and if I blink I can imagine his face when we were kids.

I wake up before sunrise, lying on top of the bedspread in my clothes. Kyle's covers are torn back. He's lying on the white sheets in his jeans and T-shirt.

I watch his chest for a full minute, not letting my head or eyes move at all, before I am sure he is breathing.

I'm not sure why he wouldn't be. It just seems important to check.

I look around the room, see my two bags strewn across the carpet.

We'd stopped for the night in Rawlins, then gone drinking at a nearby bar. My head hurts and my mouth feels thick and sticky. I go to the bathroom and drink two glasses of water, the water pouring only lukewarm from the tap.

Kyle and I used to drink, but it wasn't often that we got drunk. Drunk like that. I can't remember exactly how it happened.

And I'm thinking how I've been on my own for the last few years. Rarely getting to know other workers at farms or on construction sites. Playing pool with them in a bar, eating lunch with them in the cab of a truck. Telling stories on the back of a loading dock at night. But no one I got drunk with. No one I met who ever became anything like a friend.

I sit down again, on my bed, with a third glass of water. I take a long drink, the tepid water only adding another coat to the layers in my mouth, to the beer and sleep. It seems like Kyle and I were talking, till late, about growing up in Tacoma. It seems like we'd made some sense of things. I hear those words. *We've made some sense of things.* I hear Kyle saying that.

Although it doesn't sound like Kyle's voice. And it doesn't sound like something Kyle would say. Kyle made sense of things, but without saying it. With Kyle, there just weren't so many questions. There just weren't so many things that would happen.

I hear a car on the highway, the rush of its motion seeming to pass from room to room in the motel. And then there's no noise, no sound, no movement or motion from Kyle or the room. I look again to see if he's breathing. It just seems important to check.

We've made some sense of things.

I can't manage to think of all the places Kyle's been.

2   RETURNING

Cold air blows down her legs from the broken vent near the door. She is driving West on Interstate 80, through Nebraska, two days from Tacoma, the sun coming up in the rearview mirror. The sky above the horizon becomes a brighter gold, the deeply blue sky in the distance fading to white, the edge of the sun now rising into view behind her.

She squints her eyes so she can stare into the light in the mirror. She feels better driving. She lights a cigarette and turns on music. Her face and neck are warm, her legs cold under the air from the broken vent.

She drives for a few hours, then stops for breakfast at a restaurant near a gas station. It is early still, not even seven, and so she only locks the door, takes a seat near the window so she can watch the car.

She buys a local newspaper to read as she eats her toast and fried eggs and potatoes. With the coffee and the morning's drive, the words on the page sometimes shimmer and blur. But she reads. It keeps her from thinking too much.

And what she will think about if she looks up is the dreams, the clouds, the violence of sunlight twisting down from the sky.

Sometimes she thinks that what happened is

that she woke up too fast one day. Not yet released from the sleep. But it doesn't matter, what happened. Or why this is.

She closes her eyes and once more sees the cover lifted from her dreams, her dreams and her fear and her wishes all one thing.

She can move the clouds.

Or fly among them.

And everywhere there is the fighting. The people she can see, circling, moving, ranging closer to each other, fighting that goes on beyond what her eyes can see.

She opens her eyes as the waitress pours her more coffee.

Her brother told her stories, the two of them hiding under the sheets in his room. And now the stories have come true. Any time she closes her eyes. Any time she sleeps.

She thinks she is losing her mind.

She counts her money after she's paid the bill and gotten back in the car and checked that everything is all right. She sits in the drivers seat, counting her money and knowing the trip will cost her a few hundred dollars in food, gas and motels. Half a pay check, she is thinking. Half a pay check because of this.

And she kicks the floor and then kicks it again. The door to the restaurant opens and she can hear someone walking by, can feel the person watching her. Some tired woman in a beat up car near the highway. She wants to scream at them or to cry or just to sleep for the rest of the day.

And after a minute she starts the car and drives to the on ramp.

Because she's remembered that the job is gone, and paychecks don't matter. She'll be dead in a few months anyway.

3 NOW
WITH KYLE
TACOMA
DRIVING AWAY
RETURNING

3   NOW

The neighbor's always telling us I should join his agency, start selling real estate like him. In Missouri, he says, the test is not hard at all.

It's an easy job, he says.

And I nod, and smile, and I tell him I'm pretty happy running the lumberyard.

I don't talk much when we're with the neighbors, but they seem to like us.

We drive, the five of us, with the three kids in the back, and there are conversations about how much is infinity plus infinity. Conversations about the height of the moon. Conversations about the weight of the sun. Conversations about how, in the sunlight, there is more dust in the air than in the shade. One of the boys sneezes more in the sunlight, he says, because the sunlight attracts dust, and the other boy says it's because the dust is attracted to his nose, and the girl, the oldest, she shakes her head, trying to get my attention in the mirror, and I think I'll try to explain this all to them, but decide not to, because why does it need to be explained?

He'll know soon enough. There's so much time before he has to know.

And the kids talking will remind me of being a child, remind me of Kyle or of Teddy, and if I think of them I'll begin to try to piece it together, remember what happened, think through each moment, and I'll focus myself on getting it right, remembering it all in the or-der it happened.

But usually I can stop that. Because the order means nothing, the times and years nothing either. What matters is each moment, in any order, and the order is only a distraction meant to keep me from thinking about each thing that happened.

And I have no problem remembering each thing.

And the children will be laughing, in the back seat.

I have to make them be different than me.

3   WITH KYLE

It seemed like there was music then.

And I was looking around the car and I could see flashing lights from the sunlight outside, light caught in the insides of the Volkswagen's very flat windows and it was like I was still remembering and couldn't stop and in the reflection I could see Kyle's face, in the driver's seat, and I couldn't remember how long Kyle had been there. It'd been days, but I couldn't remember that, even though I knew it, and I thought it was because of the music. It's the music and the lights and this small car, I thought, and I turned to Kyle and saw he had his eyes closed and his face was lifting to the ceiling and the music I thought I heard was getting louder, an approaching cloud around me. And I felt myself swallow, watched Kyle and his face so stiff and hard, his head dropping slowly, mouth and eyes frozen shut, face falling and stopping only when he did open his eyes, when he had to look up at me at an angle, seeing me in the reflection of the windshield in front of us, and I saw the black-black pupils in white staring past the hard curves of his brow and Kyle, mouth open, lips barely touching as he formed words, said flatly and not that loudly but in a voice that carried through the music, "Took a while." And Kyle stared from just a few feet away, a distance doubled in the space of the reflection, and I reached and found an empty bottle, held the hard, smooth glass tightly, softness spinning in my mind, Kyle still staring without a blink, voice drained of any turn, "Took a while, Brian," he said. "The acid just took a while."

The air was cool and good in my nose and mouth and I breathed deeper, took more in. It was better now. An hour later, and we only felt good.

We were seventeen, in the winter, out near the Cispus and Cowlitz Rivers. Kyle and I had taken acid a few hours ago, driving the hard frozen roads in his old Bug, finally stopping now when Kyle said we needed to stop. The car had slowed and I was turning to him wondering why and he was smiling slightly and his eyes were wide and he took his hands from the wheel. "I think I need to take my hands from the wheel," he said and we stopped.

Grouse hunting on acid was new, and not really a great idea, given the guns. But we'd hardly ever shot the guns in four years of grouse hunting. The guns were just so loud.

I saw Kyle now with his .22 walking a few feet to my left, then standing still. The woods were very quiet and the ground was soft under my feet and the tops of the trees were a ceiling over us that let through only streaks of sunlight, light in the air around me and in front of me and beyond it all, close and far away, there were the trees in shadows, trees in bright light. Forty miles into the forest, seventy miles from anywhere, grouse country, shimmering.

We were walking through a dense line of trees and came to a fallen fir. It was five feet thick and was somehow held a few feet in the air and I was putting my gun on top of the tree, slowly climbing, the wood soft and wet even though the ground was frozen. The damp and green and black moss covering the bark was breaking off under my hands and chest as I slid then rolled over the trunk. I dropped to the soft ground on the other side, landing and bouncing and feeling very light.

I turned to look up at Kyle and he was whispering, "Wait."

He was crouching some, but stood up on the trunk. He was pointing forward. "Grouse," he said.

I turned, stared into the woods. There were few trees and little brush in the thirty yards in front of us, patches of sunlight on the ground, shining through the ceiling of branches. At the edge of the thirty yards, where the trees were dense and shimmering hard, I thought I could see a bush moving slightly.

"Grouse?" I heard myself whisper. "You saw it?"

"Yes," Kyle said.

I crouched down, feeling myself breathing very carefully, feeling myself trying to make all my movements smooth and controlled. I looked back at Kyle.

He was smiling, starting to laugh very quietly. He put his gun on the trunk. He was trying to talk but couldn't. This went on for awhile. Finally he put his hand across his face and looked at me, staring, eyes wide. "I'll flank left and take up a point at the end of this tree," he said quickly. "Once I'm in position, you fire a volley of shots into the bush. When it comes out," he said, now staring forward, "I'll shoot it."

I had to lean over, hands and knees on the ground, eyes wet. Laughing.

After a long while I nodded. I got to my feet, crouching. I put bullets in the gun. I checked that the safety was on, three times I checked.

I looked up at Kyle. He started to move down the log.

"And remember," he said, lifting his gun, "if it charges, stand your ground. You cannot outrun it."

I was back on my knees, eyes wet, trying to stop. Breathless from it all.

When I finally looked up again, Kyle had made his way out to the end of the log. I noticed again that it was suspended in the air and for a long time I wondered how. Then I put my hand across my face and started to walk forward, crouching, watching the bush. The bush was not moving and I thought maybe the grouse had run away.

I was wanting a last sip but didn't have a beer. I was wanting that taste that gives you focus, the last cold, clean drink that finishes it all, sets you on even.

I kneeled in the damp needles, brown and green under me, the smell sweet and pine, and I raised the gun to my shoulder. I was in a spot of sunlight and things outside the light were much darker than before and there was dust floating in the bright air around me. I turned to look at Kyle, saw his rifle was raised, and I turned back to the bush, could hear myself breathing and could feel the wood stock of the gun cool and smooth against my face.

I squeezed the trigger twice, the shots so loud and the gun twice kicking lightly against my shoulder. A round brown animal was running from the bush. I swung my rifle and could hear the crack of Kyle's gun and I squeezed the trigger twice again, the rifle kicking against my shoulder.

I saw the grouse fall.

"Oh my god," I said loudly.

I lowered the gun, my ears ringing, an echo of the shots still disappearing into the forest. I walked to the grouse, standing above it and watching its legs and wings jerk, seeing it again and again try to stand.

It was a fairly horrible thing to watch. I stood wincing, staring, the bird jerking, jerking, blood flying off it as it moved, spraying small drops across the needles on the ground.

There was a shot and I looked and was realizing Kyle was next to me and he'd shot the bird and killed it.

We drove more then, and I tried not to think much about the grouse.

We talked and it was hard. Not what we talked about, but the words, making sentences, forming sounds from the thoughts moving so quickly in our minds. Acid took away your speech, which was okay, just different, and there was so much else going on anyway.

I can't remember a lot of what we said. But it was good and I liked Kyle and it didn't matter that we couldn't remember what we said.

But I remember he asked me about Will Wilson. I remember that for sure. Would have, because Kyle never asked about Will Wilson or Coe or, by then, even Teddy, who he'd known too since we were little kids.

"Will Wilson was near my aunt's house the other day," I remember Kyle saying.

And that was a question. Why was he there? What was he doing? Why would he be near me?

I looked at Kyle then and it seemed like a few minutes after he'd spoken. I looked at him because I'd realized something. It was gone already, lost in flashing lights of cold sunlight through the windows, of cold air in the car, but I'd realized something. Something that, already, I couldn't see or remember.

I knew I hadn't answered his question. This wasn't what I'd realized, but I'd remembered that I was supposed to answer Kyle's question. "I don't know," I said to Kyle.

The car followed the hard narrow road to the left, sliding some on the gravel, and we were only driving these roads, not sure where we exactly were, but we drove, the car downshifting on a hill, following a curve, the deepest green, still rising along the road, through trees, trees.

The road opened onto a clear cut. A few square miles without anything. Only black, burnt stumps and branches.

The car was slowing. I think I knew it before Kyle. He was leaning forward, over the wheel, staring out, eyes moving across the black and destroyed forest. He'd shut off the engine, or it had died, and we were nearly stopped. It was so quiet, and black, and you imagined there'd been a lot of people here and large machines and a roar of engines and the smell of diesel and the force of it, not the cutting, but the force of the machines pulling, ramming, pushing at the trees, that's what you imagined.

Kyle had been talking. I wasn't sure what he'd said. His voice was quiet and I'd been staring at the black embers that covered a stump near my window. "When we fish," he was saying, "we do a lot of killing. All those fish, and the seals and porpoises that get tangled in the nets. I fish with guys who like all that killing. Even though on the boats you never talk about it, never say that you killed anything at all."

I took a drink from a beer I was holding. The bottle was cold in my hand and the beer cold on my face where it had spilt from my lips.

"Bad to have killed that grouse," I said.

"Just a bird," Kyle said. I turned to him. His face was light and moving. "More though," he said, nodding some, and smiling, "right? More?"

And I felt myself nod. And I heard him breathe deep.

"There's other kinds of killing," he said and I knew if I looked at him I'd see that he was staring at me. "What Will Wilson does is killing."

I nodded.

"No one dies," he said, "but there's just so much death."

I nodded.

"You should stop all of it," he said.

And I nodded.

"As long as you know that," he said.

And I nodded.

And I knew then that I could only stop it by leaving. And knew then that I would leave, with Kyle, another year, graduate, and we could leave, to Alaska hopefully. That's what we'd said, at least.

But I could only stop it by leaving.

We were outside of the car now and it had gotten very cold. We'd seen a frozen pond in the middle of the burn and we were sitting quietly at the edge of the ice now, the burnt remnants of the trees here coated with a layer of ice, the two of us sitting on the frozen ground, near the edge of the pond. Looking out at the broken reflection of the blue falling to orange sky. And when the sunset started with all that gold and pink and distant, dying winter light, Kyle and I were without realizing it watching dead branches creak slowly, watching cold white air blow out of our mouths like tall summer clouds. Hearing the ice in front of us seize and shift. Feeling our hearts pushing blood in easy, easy thumps. Kyle laughing quietly, in a steady, stretching calm, after I said, *It's wonderful. It really is.*

It was a few hours later that the acid went bad.

Bad because I knew, suddenly, what I'd realized. Knew what I'd realized when Kyle said Will

Wilson's name. Knew it was about the way Kyle had said it.

Kyle was not afraid of Will Wilson.

And that was worse than realizing what he'd said to me. That all of it should stop.

Kyle wasn't afraid of Will Wilson. But I was.

Kyle wasn't afraid of Will Wilson. And Will Wilson couldn't know that.

But later, when I thought about that day near the frozen pond, I would forget about how the acid went bad. I would remember only that Kyle and I had sat quietly staring at the sunset shining through the ice in the branches, the gold light turning the trees white and silver and brilliant in the air, lifting me as I breathed, as I so easily pulled in cold air and bright light, as I so freely touched that reflecting forest with every surface of my body.

Always, later, a part of me would wish I could be there again, held so still, blown through too, gold light shining in my body till I died.

For years I'd remember it that way. In Wyoming, on a farm, the end of the day, a sunset.

Sometimes still, I'd wish.

But I shouldn't have.

Kyle wasn't afraid of Will Wilson. That's all I should have remembered.

3   TACOMA

Many of the housing developments built in Tacoma in the late fifties and early sixties include small, freestanding garages behind the boxy, one-story homes. The houses are small and have one or two bedrooms and a living room and kitchen and bathroom. There are small yards in front with a narrow, straight, concrete path leading to the smoothly painted slab that serves as a small porch. Some owners plant junipers and pine trees around the homes, even flower beds and vegetable gardens. But many of the houses have little landscaping around them and stand slightly raised from the level of the street, isolated on their small bit of property. The houses are painted pale green or light blue or white, empty colors that you can't quite remember, and in some areas the houses go on for miles, twelve or fifteen of them lining one side of a street.

Maybe because they're too small to park in or too far from the house, the garages in back often stand unused – the swinging door left open, the small panes of the windows broken by neighborhood kids.

Starting when we were seventeen, Will Wilson, Coe, Teddy and I would burn these garages down. At two or three in the morning, we'd sneak along a dark alley with a can of gasoline, pouring it against the inside base of the wooden walls, making a big pool in the center of the smooth, concrete slab. The four of us throwing matches at the gas, each glancing around at the alley and the surrounding houses, the garage igniting in front of us like an oven, the walls burning with low flames, the pool in the center burning three feet high.

We burned nine of the garages in the fall and winter that year. By the sixth one, in January, we made the newspaper, a small article about what fire officials believed was a pattern of arson. The police had been consulted. Officers on patrol in Tacoma's North End would be checking alleys.

Will Wilson came to my house that day with the article, smiling as I read it. And that Friday the four of us bought thin, black ski masks and cheap black gloves at the B&I, and we went out at night and burned two more garages, all of us smiling through our mouth holes, bouncing on the balls of our feet as we thought about police cruisers racing down the gravel alley, hitting their blue and gold lights and shining a spotlight in our direction, having to chase us over fences and through yards.

But no one saw us that night. There was another article in the paper the following day, although this one was very short, no comments from fire or police officials. And then the next Friday at two a.m., when we went out in our masks and gloves and found a garage on Cheyenne Street only ten blocks from the last garage we'd burned, after we'd just poured the center pool of gas and were stepping out of the garage, crouching behind the garbage cans in the alley as Will Wilson and me took matches from our pockets, then a white patrol car did turn down the alley and did hit its lights. Some neighbor had seen us. Had called the police.

And the pool of gas was bursting yellow, blue and white.

It took a few minutes to realize how angry the city had been about us burning down two garages in one night after that first article in the paper. In those few minutes after the patrol car turned the corner – as the four of us were sprinting away from the glow and smoke of the fire, running through a yard and across a street into another yard and into and then down an alley and onto another street – we saw three more cop cars, unmarked brown and blue and white cruisers, all moving at high speed, squealing their tires and running their engines full out.

I was sprinting with Will Wilson in front of me and Teddy beside and Coe just a few steps behind, ducking under the branches of a tree, bouncing off a fence as we ran between a house and a tall row of hedges.

I thought about how we could go to jail.

And still I was smiling like the three of them. There was no way we'd get caught.

Two cruisers with their lights flashing were turning corners, an unmarked car flew down an alley we'd been about to enter, sirens blew some-where to our left. I saw at the end of one street two uniformed cops carrying flashlights, both hustling across a lawn toward us.

We would find out later that there were ten cars involved, both fire and police units.

Will Wilson turned to look at us without breaking his stride, his face so happy through the eye holes of his mask. He only said, "Split up. Find the gulch." And he turned left down an alley toward an oncoming cruiser, his thin body just black in the light of the blue and gold flashers and white headlights. Coe ran right, down the alley and away from the car, and I jumped through the bush in front of me, landing on a soft, damp lawn, Teddy rolling on the ground behind me.

And from that oncoming cruiser I heard a voice on a speaker blaring at Will Wilson. *"Okay, kid, stop. Okay, stop. Stop. Oh shit, Karl, turn."*

Teddy and I were running, ducking between houses and hedges, between cars parked on the street. Lights were coming on in some houses and a few people stood on porches, looking for the cop cars, listening to the engines and sirens a few blocks away, in front of us and behind.

Teddy and I were circling back across Huson Street, then Ferdinand, Mullen, finally reaching a house facing Cheyenne, the street where we'd started, just two blocks away from the garage we'd burned. Only two blocks closer to the gulch. We were kneeling next to a house, sucking breaths and shaking some and looking back down the street. Two fire trucks and a fire chief's car were parked in front of the house with the garage. Yellow and red lights flashed, a small crowd of firefighters and neighbors stood together talking.

An unmarked car came racing down Cheyenne. A cruiser with lights and no siren came from the other direction. The gulch was just four blocks away on the other side of Cheyenne. But Cheyenne was wider and better lit than most streets and between it and the gulch there were other very brightly lit streets. And so Teddy and I decided to run parallel to Cheyenne, going two blocks to Sherman Elementary before crossing the dark school grounds to the gulch.

We were running down an alley, slowing in the shadows before entering a street, when from my right a man with no shirt nearly tackled Teddy. Teddy and I were running forward and looking back, seeing this guy where he'd fallen, seeing him now standing up. No shoes or pants – a neighbor in his underwear. We reached the next alley and were sprinting through shallow puddles and in his bare feet this guy had to slow because of the rocks.

I was thinking that if he'd gotten hold of Teddy, I would have hit the man. Not in the face. In the back maybe, so that he wouldn't see me swing. But again and again. Until he let go.

Teddy and I turned left into a yard and away from Cheyenne and the gulch. We hopped two fences before turning toward the school, now a half block away. We cut across mostly dark lawns, running as close to the houses as the shrubs and porches allowed. In the yards with no landscaping we ran crouched over, trying to find shadows. The sirens were behind us and didn't seem to be coming close and we ran without seeing a cop car or any more neighbors.

We climbed over a fence and landed behind a tall, two-story wooden building that had been home to the Boys Club when I was a little kid but that had been sold off since then. We kneeled near the corner of the building, heaving in breaths and looking out on Cheyenne. There were no cars moving and no people at all.

"Shit, shit, shit," Teddy was saying. "Shit, shit, shit." And we were both scared, but we were smiling. We'd always wanted to be chased.

The edge of the dirt soccer field at Sherman Elementary was on the opposite corner. Beyond the field were the big log toys and the swing sets and the large, tall set of monkey bars that kids had called the skyscraper because it was rectangular and as tall as the school building. Behind all that was the long, one-story, L-shaped school, some classrooms dimly lit, the insides of the windows covered with paper snowmen and Santa faces. Sherman and its field and playgrounds covered about three whole blocks, most of it bordered by a high, chain-link fence.

Teddy and I were still breathing hard, speaking to each other in short, quiet bursts, quickly deciding to cross the empty but brightly lit Cheyenne intersection, slide under the chain-link fence that bordered the street, then run along the fence toward the cafeteria at the right side of the building. Just a block behind the cafeteria, on the other side of another brightly lit street, was the gulch. We could even see the white wood and concrete barrier that ran along the gulch's edge, the white paint turned nearly blue under the streetlights.

And so we crossed the street and slid under the chain-link fence and we were running across the dark long-jump pit when three cars with their head-lights off came from the corner near the gulch, the corner we were running toward, and we stopped to turn back and there was an unmarked car on Cheyenne that must have seen us crossing, that had maybe seen us kneeling next to the old Boys Club building, had maybe called in the three dark cars.

We turned toward the other end of the L-shaped building, where the two-story-high gym was, but we had to run the width of the soccer field, a wide-open sprint that still took us no closer to the gulch. Spotlights were beaming out of the cars be-hind us, flashing on the dirt to our right and left and now Teddy's running body lit up brightly. It was the spotlight from the unmarked car on Chey-enne, now cruising slowly down the street, parallel to us.

"Stop there," a voice screeched.

I could hear the high roar of the engines be-hind us and as we ran I looked back and saw that two cars, both cruisers, had pulled onto the dirt soccer field, their headlights shining and flashers spinning, both tearing across the field, two trails of dust kicked twenty feet high behind them. The Cheyenne car had sped up and turned in at the end of the fence near the gym, the spotlight bright in our eyes and I could see that a door was opening. An officer was running toward us.

"Climb the bars," I yelled, my cheeks and jaw rubbing against the scratchy, damp material of the mask.

We'd reached the asphalt near the swing set and we veered slightly to the right and the cop from the unmarked car was near us, his pale, sweating face smiling and Teddy and I both jumped at a run onto the monkey bars and I smacked my forehead on a bar but we were scrambling up, the cop for just a second getting his hand on my leg.

The two cars from the field were grinding to a stop and I heard, "You stupid fucks!" from the cop below and an electronic voice was squealing, *"Now stop! Stop up there!"*

We were just reaching the top of the bars when I glanced down and the one who'd almost grabbed me was leaning and breathing and two others were out of the cars, strutting slow, and the cloud of dust from the two cruisers was passing around us, choking our air at the top of the monkey bars.

I don't know who decided to build that set of monkey bars so tall and so close to the building, but I'm sure the teachers and principal curse that man or woman every day. Any kid who went to Sherman Elementary knew that if you were careful and kept your balance and got up enough speed as you stepped across the top bars, then you could, even as a child, jump from the monkey bars to the school's roof. When I was a kid at Sherman, a teacher had to act as monkey bar monitor during recess, standing at the bars every day, watching for some kid to get up the nerve to jump across. Even with the monitor, it happened about once a month. About twice a year, a kid missed and broke an arm or leg.

Teddy and I landed on our feet, bouncing on the roof's soft, spongy surface. We were halfway down the roof before I heard the car tires grinding in the dirt of the soccer field and saw the spotlights and flashlights shining up toward the sky, the narrow, white beams moving back and forth as if signaling the grand opening of a store.

I looked back and saw a cop had climbed the monkey bars, one arm hooked firmly in a top bar, waving his flashlight across the roof where we'd landed. But Teddy and I were already near the bend in the building, running crouched low behind the rows of tall, metal vent hoods and boxy air conditioning units.

I knew at least two cars were circling the building and I remembered there was another car that hadn't sped after us across the field. It could be anywhere. And more cars were probably on the way.

We turned right at the bend, both of us running toward the cafeteria.

"Kindergarten to the alley?" Teddy asked between breaths and I nodded and he turned and ran toward the edge of the building and Teddy jumped the eight feet over the small covered area where the kindergartners played, on the alley side of the high chain-link fence that bordered the school.

We were less than one block from the gulch.

And as I jumped from the roof I slipped, landed on the fence not over it, catching my fingers in the steel links and tearing open the skin and it was a second before I could climb and Teddy was looking back at me and yelling that the cops were behind me, right behind me, and I dropped sideways from the top of the fence as it began to shake from a cop climbing. I landed on my side and was standing when I saw a cop car coming down the alley and I was following Teddy through the yard of a house, climbing a wooden fence and stepping across a row of garbage cans, the last can falling behind me. Teddy was ahead of me as we ran down the sloping front yard, stepping between rose bushes and junipers, what sounded like three cops behind us, night sticks and walkie-talkies and guns all creaking and bouncing in their belts. Sirens were screaming close to the right, and beyond Teddy was the bright street bordered by the low white wall at the edge of the gulch, the gulch that here was more open and visible than anywhere else in Tacoma, sweeping in an arc a half-mile around, sloping a few hundred yards deep like a quilt of thick, dark green trees and bushes, stretching two miles or more, uninterrupted till it reached the waterfront, the gulch here forming an amphitheater looking out on the bay and the glow of lights from the unseen mills on the Tide Flats some five miles away where right then my dad was working, and as I ran across the street with a cop car skidding to a stop near me, both doors opening, men jumping out, I saw Browns Point across the just shimmering water of the bay, its very distant lighthouse slowly spinning in the night.

I do remember wondering if the police would shoot an arsonist.

There are many steep but manageable trails into the gulch from the top of that wide ridge along the street. But Teddy and I weren't near any of them. The cops were behind us and coming from the sides, yelling for us to stop and the sounds of engines were coming close from somewhere to the left and the lights of the skid-stopped car were reflecting off Teddy's head and Teddy seemed to be swinging his head like he was looking for a trail and he was screaming, "Fuck, man, fuck!" and as he hesitated that bit I caught up and screamed "Just go!" and stepped at a run onto the top of the fence, Teddy then next to me, the two of us jumping feet first over the ridge and into the gulch below.

It was four long, silent seconds before I was sure I'd hit ground. And that ground was steep and rough against my back and butt and I was sliding hard down the slope, grinding across wet rocks and dirt and my feet were hitting roots and trunks and I slid on into the dark, one hand to the side, desperately trying to keep myself sliding feet first and not on my side or chest, the other arm protecting my face, and even then the branches tore off my mask. And finally I slowed some and caught onto the trunk of a tree growing out from the side of the hill. Rocks and dirt and a bottle hit me in the back, falling from above me. I could feel both hands were bleeding. Feel that my jeans had torn through to the skin in two places. I looked up and I'd slid a couple hundred feet, the white fence not visible, the only sign of the street the narrow brightness of a distant flashlight shining through the leaves.

I found Teddy another hundred feet down, in the nearly total darkness where the steepness of the slope had lessened. I'd cut my leg and my hands were ground black with dirt and blood. Through the shadows I could see Teddy's round face. Curly hair standing high off his head. He'd lost or taken off his mask. I heard him quietly laughing in starts and trying to take big breaths as he held onto the branches. I sat there next to him, breathing hard. Nodding absently as if I were answering questions. I thought I could hear the sounds of a radio above us. I looked up and through the branches and leaves I could see pinholes of light flickering – flashlights and spotlights pointing over the edge.

Teddy was laughing evenly now. He touched my forehead with his gloved hand, and I could see his teeth shining white in the dark. "You're bleeding," Teddy said. "I heard the crunch when you hit that monkey bar."

Teddy wasn't cut or even bruised.

We slid another fifty feet, then were able to walk on the now barely steep slope. It took half an hour of walking through bushes and trees and deep mud puddles before we found a trail. In another half an hour, we found the small utility sheds where the four of us often went.

Teddy and I climbed onto a roof and didn't talk much, only smiling some and nodding and seeming to still concentrate on our breathing.

"Very fun," I said once. And we nodded and

smiled wider.

After a few minutes Teddy leaned back and seemed to fall asleep. I knew that really he was trying to breathe slowly and was crying some into his arm. He was just having trouble winding down.

I glanced at him only a few times. His soft face, his somehow young, almost puffy body. In Tacoma, it was a softness some people mistook for weakness. If the four of us got into a fight, Teddy was often singled out, approached first. But Teddy fought harder than any stranger who ever tried him. The softness in his face never diminishing as he circled slowly, swung hard, beat some kid bloody on the ground. Beat some kid and seemed to like it. Because Teddy was, in so many ways, as empty as the rest of us. Driven by the same desires. Wanting so badly to have control. Wanting so much of what he'd otherwise never get.

But he had that soft face. Soft even then, seventeen, years into our addiction to it all. Soft and I'd known him so long, we'd been kids once, and it made him different.

Coe showed up half an hour later. His low, heavy shape appearing from behind a row of trees. He'd run about six blocks from where we'd first split up, ducking between houses before climbing into an unlocked car in an alley. He lay on the floor for an hour, hearing the sirens fade and come close, cars passing down the alley, some racing, some moving slow with their spotlights lingering. But when he got out of the car, he was able to walk through the shadows of houses and alleys. He only had to cross one bright street, climbing into the gulch at a main trail about a half mile from where Teddy and I had jumped. He said he saw cop cars there, three of them, flashers spinning, shining their spotlights into the gulch. But the police didn't see him. Didn't chase him. I think he was a little let down.

After another hour, I was starting to worry about Will Wilson not being back yet. I didn't say that to Coe or Teddy. But they were worried too, I was sure. Worried that if Will Wilson was caught and arrested and sent to the jail for juveniles, then Will Wilson would, for some amount of time, be gone. And nights like this wouldn't happen again until he got out.

But as the sky was turning gray with the sunrise, someone tugged on my foot and Coe and I jumped up, yelling.

Will Wilson was smiling. Somehow seeming so thin in the dark. A bare, hard person springing up next to me on the shed.

I almost didn't believe how far he'd run. Circling about a mile and a half before he could begin to come back. The police had been within blocks, sometimes feet, the whole way. Two patrol cars and four unmarked cars circled his area, spotlights shining, sirens blaring. Sometimes rolling dark and quiet down streets he crossed. They would spot him and he would disappear, sliding under parked cars, stepping into empty garages, mostly running in the shadows. He crossed the football fields at Mason Junior High and thought he'd lost them. But they caught sight and he had to run through front and backyards with the police behind him on foot, three of them crossing the wooden foot bridge over a section of gulch as Will Wilson looped back to the Proctor Bridge where two cars were waiting. He ducked down at the edge of the bridge to the dirt ledge where we drank, then jumped off the ledge and into the fifty-foot dirt slope. But the three cops came sliding down behind him, running with flashlights shining as he sprinted down a bottom trail in the gulch. He couldn't duck or hide, they were too close. And so he ran on a quarter mile, then turned up a steep trail. Trying simply to outrun them. Halfway up, he did. The police dropped off and Will Wilson kept on, finally getting far enough ahead that he could cut off into the bushes, circling slowly and quietly back to the bottom. Hearing cops swearing and breathing as they walked back toward the bridge.

Coe and Teddy and I told Will Wilson our stories and the four of us found a few old, warm beers in one of the sheds and shared them. We walked home with the sun coming up, staying in the gulch as long as possible, then crossing through alleys to Will Wilson's house, where we could all change clothes.

And, of course, I didn't say anything about Teddy crying.

We never burned another garage. It was the middle of my last winter with them, but there were, still, some limits.

Which isn't true, really. Not at all. The only reason we stopped is that it wasn't worth the chance of being caught. Because, right then, there were just so many other things we still wanted to do.

•

We started breaking into houses simply to see what would happen. We kept doing it because there was no good reason to stop.

We did it first on a Friday when we were sixteen and Will Wilson had told Coe and Teddy and me to wear dark clothes out that night. We drove with Will Wilson to the nicest neighborhood of Tacoma's North End, Old Town, an area we often drove through, looking at the wealthiest houses in Tacoma, imagining what it felt like to live there. This Friday around midnight Will Wilson pulled his cousin's big, tan Buick down a narrow road to a small park and stopped the car behind a clean and hidden city dumpster. We got out and followed Will Wilson into an entrance to the gulch we'd never seen, ducking under the branches still wet from that day's rain, feeling under our feet the soft mud that sometimes didn't dry, even in the summer, because of the trees overhead. We came out of the gulch in the backyard of a tall, white house.

"We're going inside," Will Wilson said, crouching behind a damp row of junipers.

I remember I understood right away that we weren't doing this to steal. But Coe asked if we were taking things and Teddy was just scared, saying to me, "I don't know. What do you think, Brian? Brian, what do you think?"

That Teddy would doubt Will Wilson in front of us all showed how scared he was. Will Wilson with his lean face, his brown hair to his shoulder blades, his neck always tilted, pulled tight. And so when I think about that first break-in now, I know Teddy was less scared about what would happen to us in that house than about what we might do inside.

This night Will Wilson only smiled at Teddy, said, "We're just going to see what happens." We crossed the soft lawn and Will Wilson led us to a side door that was hidden from the road, touched the knob and this was the North End of Tacoma, so the door was unlocked. We passed through the entrance into darkness, saw the black shapes of unseen furniture, gray light from a window. Felt beneath our feet a wood floor, then carpet. Around us was the full and spreading silence and we couldn't then explain it, could only sense it and want it, but from that first moment the break-ins were about the violation itself, the entering of a space that wasn't ours, that was protected not by guns or bars or even locks, but by an assumption of safety. An assumption that we – with one easy motion – had taken hold of and ended.

And that first time, like most every time that followed, we smiled knowing that the owners and their children were upstairs asleep.

We taught ourselves to pick locks when we had to, to force open windows. Quietly, quickly. Without damage. We went into two-story houses in Old Town, Fircrest, even out in Gig Harbor – all the nicest areas we knew of. Nicest anywhere. Nicest possible.

Inside, Coe's low, heavy body moved so gracefully in the dark, silently bouncing on couches, stretching out easily on carpets, walking quietly across dining room tables. Coe tried sometimes to circle a room without stepping on the floor, hiking up his badly fitting jeans as he noiselessly leapt from piano bench to radiator to a TV on a rolling stand that he used to pull himself three feet before the cord went tight. And only when he seemed on the verge of thrashing about and finally making noise, did Will Wilson step in front of him and grab his face at the jaw, shake it, *No.*

Often the four of us didn't even let out whispers, just moved our lips or pointed.

Teddy liked to stand at a window. With his curly hair turned gray in the darkness, his soft and round face turned pale by a streetlight outside, Teddy always looked like an aging man. Some old guy at his window. With nothing to do but stare. At first I thought Teddy was watching for the police. But one time he told me he was just seeing what this family looked at during the day.

Will Wilson liked to go through cabinets, sometimes drawers, seeming to count the soup cans, the forgotten records and books. The neatly folded t-shirts and socks.

But the four of us left the houses almost completely undisturbed. Even Coe was always careful to return furniture to its place. I think the owners woke up in the morning and never knew anything had happened, maybe wondered weeks or months later, How long has that lamp shade been crooked? Is this where I left my shoes?

And in those years afterward, working, if I found myself telling stories about Tacoma, I would always think about the first break-ins. I wouldn't talk about them, but, in a bar telling some story about car tag or driving fast, I would think about the break-ins, and I would I know that what I'd liked most was watching the three of them in a house that was ours. I bounced soundlessly on chairs playing tag with Coe, stood next to Teddy staring out at the night, searched through closets and drawers with a smiling Will Wilson. But I now mostly remember watching through the shadows, seeing my three friends doing a careful and silent nighttime dance.

Sometimes the four of us entered a house and people were out of their bedrooms. We heard them upstairs, the ceiling creaking and the four of us stood still, the first times frightened, later smiling. We never said so, but we always wanted to be chased from a house. Sometimes we saw people asleep in front of flashing TVs. Saw them from the shadows as they crossed to the kitchen, then turned and tiredly mounted the stairs.

One time someone sat in the living room darkness watching the four of us wander through the house and she didn't say a word and we didn't notice her till I was climbing out the window, looking back, seeing a silhouette staring from a far corner chair. Scared.

We broke into houses after nights when the boredom had overwhelmed us, sometimes too after fun nights with parties and long and fast drives. We sometimes planned on break-ins, other times seemed not to talk about it till we were parking the car, looking for an entrance. Though, thinking back on those unplanned times it now seems as if somewhere in someone's mind, probably Will Wilson's, there had been one goal all along.

And Will Wilson and I, after two years of break-ins where we stayed on the first floor, when we were eighteen we walked slowly up the stairs, Will Wilson above me waving me up with his hand, the two of us then sliding so carefully down a hall, passing silent and snoring doors, till near the end we heard a man and woman having sex, whining and gasping, Will Wilson and me standing outside their open door, listening through it all. Will Wilson near my face, smiling at me in the darkness.

•

Starting when we were twelve, the four of us would get girls to go down to the gulch under the Proctor Bridge or even go into the gulch as far as the abandoned utility sheds halfway between Proctor and the waterfront. Lots of kids went into the gulch, but few of them went very deep into the woods. And of those that did, none knew their way around like the four of us. And so girls went with us like it was some kind of adventure. Smiling and talking to each other, holding their book bags and sacks of pop from the Seven-Eleven, the girls would sometimes agree to go with us. Two or three, maybe four of them. Girls at school, girls walking home. Girls playing at the park on weekends.

Will Wilson just had that way.

It was enough sometimes to play hide and seek. Paired up with a girl, you would go running off to hide and, supposedly, find another couple. Really, the pairs just went off to kiss and touch. Except, at first, I didn't ever kiss a girl. I didn't know how and was embarrassed to try. So instead I would circle through the gulch, this confused girl following as I looked for the others. I would spy on Will Wilson kissing a girl in a long, unbroken hold, or Coe trying to kiss a girl heavily behind a utility building, or Teddy sitting close to his girl and kissing her lightly on the cheek.

We'd play strip poker, too. When they lost during the games of strip poker, the girls would usually take off a shoe lace or a sock. Teddy and I did about the same, not wanting to strip either. But sometimes Will Wilson and Coe would take off their shirts and jeans, as quickly as possible stripping down to their boxers. The girls would sometimes like this and laugh.

And then Will Wilson would smile and dress and once he had his shirt and jeans back on, then he'd tell these girls that we were going to leave them down here, down in the gulch until it got dark, unless they took off their shirts and bras. Angry and calling us assholes or scared and not speaking, some would start to unbutton their shirts. Will

Wilson would laugh then, and say no. He'd laugh, saying he was joking. He'd laugh as the girls started swearing at him and at us. And he'd laugh, too, but quietly, slowing now, everything slowing, as they'd start to laugh too and, sometimes, they would slowly unclip their bras and carefully lift their shirts, and they'd show us their breasts and, sometimes, we'd all be paired off again, in the woods, in the dirt, under trees, kissing. Just kissing, touching some, under the trees in the gulch.

•

I was sitting with Will Wilson in his mother's car, the two of us sharing a plastic bottle of bourbon. We were parked in a small lot next to the Narrows Bridge. He'd called me and said he wanted to go for a drive.

We were fourteen.

Above us was the dark underside of the tall, mile-long Narrows Bridge, the broad arches lifting and falling, thin cables dropping to the slightly curved surface of the road.

"We were watching TV in the camper," Will Wilson said, smiling. "Laying on the bed. I just started touching her."

I pictured Jodi, probably wearing like always jeans and a t-shirt. A girl who played in the gulch with us, who was a tough kid. Took shit from no one, laughed all night from the center of a party. So many of the boys – kids our age and hers – wanted her to be their girlfriend. Most of them said she was a tease, that she would talk to them and be nice but didn't want them as boyfriends. But if at school or parties any boys started trying something with her, Jodi would find Will Wilson. Stand with him. Maybe hold his hand. And boys wouldn't try anything after they knew she was Will Wilson's family.

She was twelve years old then, when Will Wilson and I stared out at the light over the Narrows Straight, the gold and blue sky shining bright beyond the gray and white clouds of an approaching Pacific storm. Jodi Robart. His step-dad's niece.

"She's always liked me," Will Wilson said. "And she was laughing at first. I touched her sides and legs and she was laughing."

I heard the cars, distant and loud, moving above us across the bridge.

"I can't believe we weren't doing it already," he said, squeezing the plastic bottle above his lean, smiling face, forcing yellow and warm bourbon into his mouth.

And I was nervous. Even scared. And excited.

"She fought some," he said, voice so slow, eyes so happy. "And laughed some, and finally she was just real easy under me. Real still and easy," he said, words coming now as quiet, happy hits from his throat. "I had her there naked," he said, turning to me. "I didn't see why I shouldn't. I had her there naked and I just got inside her."

It was a few weeks later that he called me. "Come over and see her," he said on the phone.

I took the city bus the four stops to his house. Feeling awkward. Feeling myself breathing carefully.

Will Wilson let me in the front door and Jodi was sitting on the couch reading a book. We were all wearing jeans and white t-shirts. Will Wilson and I started watching TV. Jodi didn't look at us.

Jodi didn't have a mom that I knew of and her dad was often out of town for six months at a time, working construction jobs at Navy bases in the Pacific. So Jodi had lived at Will Wilson's off and on for years. For the past three weeks, he'd been having sex with her every day, every day telling a silent Coe, Teddy and me about it at the waterfront.

She was a pretty girl, feathered brown hair parted down the middle.

"Let's play a game," Will Wilson said, standing and looking at Jodi.

She didn't look at him, but in a moment she stood up and followed Will Wilson outside.

In the backyard Will Wilson was smiling and Jodi had no expression. She crossed her arms over her chest and looked down at the ground. The three of us stood on the cracked patio, Will Wilson looking from her to me.

"Hide and seek," he said and pushed his long hair out of his eyes, over his ears. Even then he had such a hard, sharp face. Skin that didn't at all look soft, a face that had no baby fat left. "You two try to find me. Why don't you wait in the camper till I hide," he said. "Count to fifty. Slow. By ones."

And when Jodi and I were in there, I even started to count.

She had her arms crossed, was looking at the

floor. She hadn't said a word.

Green astro-turf carpet. A tiny sink, small cabinets. Thick, brown curtains over the scratched plastic windows.

Jodi Robart was a loud girl, funny. But I told myself girls just weren't themselves for this.

I got real close to her and she didn't move and I wasn't sure if I should talk to her or touch her or grab her.

"I know," she said, not looking up at me, walking a few steps away then turning back. "I know," she said.

The curtains were pulled away from some windows and I figured Will Wilson was watching.

I was staring at Jodi. She hadn't run.

I stepped over to her and tried to kiss her but when I got close to her face she looked up and watched as I moved closer and I didn't know how to kiss her. In the gulch the girls had always kissed me. And so I didn't know how to hold my lips, what to do with my tongue. I pulled back. She uncrossed her arms.

I was embarrassed, could feel my face turning red.

She stared. Pale eyes, squarish, pretty face.

I kept thinking, She hasn't tried to run. I kept thinking, Will Wilson must be watching.

I put my hand on her chest, feeling her bra and breasts under her t-shirt. She just watched my hand. I put my hands up her shirt and then down her pants and she just watched my arms moving. Staring at them. Uncrossing then recrossing her arms as I pulled up her shirt and unzipped her pants.

And we were laying on the small foam bed, her t-shirt around her neck and bra undone. Jeans and panties pulled down. My jeans unzipped. And it took a minute to get inside her and when I did she let out a high breath, and I was breathing hard and trying to find some rhythm but felt myself awkwardly jerking forward and she was breathing harder then and putting her arms around my neck and back and she had them there and was breathing with my breathing and rocking with my moving and I said to her quietly, "You like it, then, don't you? You do like it."

And she was breathing loud and moving with me, pushing against me, whispering in a long, deep, emptying breath, "No, I really don't."

I had sex with her five times in the next few weeks. Always in the camper with Will Wilson outside. Jodi always starting with her arms across her chest.

I never did kiss her.

Coe had sex with her, too. And Teddy. All our first times. All in that camper in Will Wilson's backyard. Before any of us turned fifteen.

"Same girl," Will Wilson was saying at the waterfront train tracks, the four of us drinking and Teddy quietly answering questions about his half hour in the camper with Jodi. His first time. "Same girl," Will Wilson was saying.

And Teddy had drunk ten or more shots from a plastic bottle of tequila, had steadily finished a half case of beer, drinking so much that Will Wilson insisted Teddy drive. Will Wilson sat in the passenger seat, grabbing the wheel when the car veered toward a curb. Pushing the gas when Teddy's foot slid off the pedal. Hitting Teddy in the arm and saying, "Wake up, little man. Wake up." And Teddy would grab the wheel and gun the gas and the car lurched forward, maybe thirty miles an hour, then just fifteen, doing this along a few miles of side roads before he started to vomit, blowing alcohol and a mess of half-digested food all down his front and lap, his chin bouncing on his chest and his hands falling off the wheel and in the back seat Coe was slapping me on the shoulder, laughing hard and jerking around and I just smiled some and watched Teddy vomit again, seeing Will Wilson smile wide, steering the car, saying so sweetly, "Hit the gas, Ted. Come on little lover, press harder on the gas."

•

The Puyallup Fair came only once a year, in September offering two weeks of roller coaster rides and horse races, livestock competitions and craft shows, all of which drew tens of thousands of people a day from Tacoma and all the small farming towns around Puyallup. Companies let employees out early and schools had entire days off so that students could go to the fair.

And that day, a day early in our senior year, when Will Wilson, Coe and Teddy and me drove

along the river to Puyallup, when the morning
sunshine turned the fall air just cooler than cold in
Will Wilson's white and bare Falcon, we all smiled.
We smiled about the fair, but smiled because we'd
started our last year of high school. Smiled because
that summer just ended we'd made good money on
the Tide Flats, more than four thousand each, working all day and night, seven days a week in warehouses or on the docks. Starting when I was twelve,
every Friday my dad had left money for me inside
the front cover of the phone book, money that I had
to live on for a week. Groceries, lunches, dinners.
Even when he was out of work, out sometimes for
a few months at a time because of changes in oil
prices, even then my dad had that money there for
me, part cash, maybe a check, in the bad times food
stamps. When work was good, my dad would buy
groceries, those weeks he'd even cook something
like a roast and potatoes for the two of us. But usually there was just the phone book money, money
that I could spend on things like a movie or Cokes
and Cheetos, but that I had to budget tight or by the
end of the week I'd be eating bologna and bread or
nothing at all.

But now, sitting in the passenger seat and leaning against the door, I looked at Will Wilson driving
and Coe and Teddy in the back seat, the river and
farms passing in the windows behind their heads,
and I now remember feeling somehow taller, somehow bigger. Thinking they looked that way, too.
My hands were thick from working and I could picture each check I'd cashed that summer, getting the

money back in twenties and hundreds and keeping it in an empty shoebox under my bed, counting it every few days. We could buy ourselves good used cars now, cars like Will Wilson's clean Falcon, could buy good quarter ounces of indoor grown pot instead of nickel bags of shake. Could buy glass liters of Wild Turkey and Cuervo instead of plastic pints of Tennessee Sam's or Sunnytime Sunrise. We were in Tacoma and it felt good. Going to the fair on fair day, when all the high schools would be there. Going to the fair where we'd gone every year since we were children, even back in those years before we knew each other, which then seemed to me like a long time ago. We were in Tacoma and now with money. Knowing things we couldn't explain. Things we could only feel.

That year we would believe Tacoma was ours.

The four of us bought the fair burgers with their mounds of fried onions, bought french fries and Cokes. We played the coin toss games, throwing two dollars, three dollars, five dollars each in dimes and nickels and quarters. Tossing them into the stacks of Seven-Up glasses and Budweiser ashtrays. The Rainier beer mugs and Coca-Cola goblets. We played the hoop toss games, threw darts at balloons. Shot pellet guns at the metal faces of Lenin and Stalin, shot at small cannons painted with the hammer and sickle. We won rubber snakes and t-shirts, won plastic beer mugs printed with Coors and Miller. Won mirrors painted with the Rolling Stones' red tongue, The Who's British flag, Led Zeppelin's falling Icarus. Coe and Teddy filled paper bags with it all, both keeping every item they won. Will Wilson, though, always traded up, three mugs for a mirror, two mirrors for a hat, three hats for a long sleeve t-shirt. And then he would give the shirt to Coe or Teddy, whichever wanted it, or to some girl watching us. And I copied him, began to trade up, gave what I won to Teddy if he wanted it, or to Coe. Or to some girl or kid watching the four of us spend money.

It was fun to win, but it was better not to have to carry anything.

We ate popcorn and hot dogs in the covered food court with its concrete floor and hundreds of plastic chairs and cafeteria benches, its high walls painted with mural-sized ads from the Sixties. Bright and sterile scenes of very blonde women. Damp bottles of Pepsi-Cola. A very cute Volkswagen Beetle.

We bought more Cokes to mix with the Jack Daniels we'd brought in small metal flasks. Drank the whiskey and Coke outside, a breeze blowing through the packed fairgrounds, carrying the smells of candied apples and hot dogs, the sounds of happily screaming children, the metallic banging and whirring of the diesel-driven rides. The distant howls of the people high up on the old wooden roller coaster, the crash as its cars jerked hard into turns.

Often we walked beneath the strings of flashing lights and the vinyl roofs of the small game tents, so that although we were outside, I remember during much of that day that I felt enclosed.

We walked in the shadow of the roller coaster's white wooden scaffolding, or the concrete and steel grandstand where The Beach Boys would play that afternoon. Or we walked in the shadow of the loud rides like the Zipper with its steel cages whipping around, the Toboggan with its cars moving at a turquoise blur.

The four of us went on the bumper cars, the only ride that Will Wilson liked. It was almost two o'clock and there was a line of people waiting, but the four of us paid the two attendants ten dollars each to stay in our cars for five rounds, to not stop us when we teamed up on the people we didn't like. Junior high kids trying to tap their girlfriends' car. High school kids and older who thought they could be a bumper car renegade. We crashed into them all, Will Wilson getting his car up to seemingly impossible speeds, ramming into strangers, jerking them violently in their seats.

In our last round, Will Wilson blindsided Coe so hard that Coe, who was not wearing his nylon safety strap, flew out of his car and landed on the metal floor. I had to crash head-on into a wall to avoid running him over, laughing so hard I couldn't steer, even as Teddy smashed me in the side, my shins cracking against my car's stiff fiberglass body, spinning away from the wall now, Will Wilson coming out of a wide, sling-shotting turn to hit me from behind, my head snapping back against the thinly padded steel pole, then whip-lashing forward so that my chest hit the steering wheel, it's steel edge bruising a rib, the heavily padded center knocking the wind out of me. I couldn't breathe but was laughing still, bouncing aimlessly through the mess of cars, out of the corner of my damp eyes seeing Will Wilson swinging out of a turn, gaining speed in the curve, pressed back from his wheel as he once again bore down on me.

After the bumper cars Coe and Teddy wanted to go on more rides, but Will Wilson wanted to walk around. And so I went off with him.

He was happy. Smiling and pointing at the people draped in fair t-shirts and hats, the ones wearing the headbands and handkerchiefs they'd won at the games. "Fair groupies," Will Wilson called them.

We walked through the crowds, seeing little kids with their parents. Seeing the high school and junior high kids in denim coats, nylon wind breakers. Many wearing high school sweatshirts and letterman's jackets. Truman, Mason, Jason Lee, Lincoln, Stadium, Puget Sound. Teenage kids in two's and four's, sometimes groups of ten or more. Usually all boys or all girls, all of them looking for girls or boys to meet.

Lots of the guys walked with their shoulders back, trying to prove themselves cool and tough. Will Wilson and I threw coins at the backs of their heads. Not wanting a fight. Just wanting to stop their silly strut.

Will Wilson talked about his mom and step-dad and how they were glad he'd made money that summer, glad he was now working on the Tide Flats on weekends and after school. How because of that they were treating him better, giving him more leeway. Not yelling at him so often, not questioning him when they'd found a bottle of bourbon in his room. In their eyes, Will Wilson said, he was an adult.

Will Wilson bought us both scones – the jelly-filled biscuits that people always lined up for at the fair – and he wouldn't take the money I held out for my share. Will Wilson had never bought something for me. Sometimes Teddy and I would lend each other money on our own. But each of the four of us always paid his own way, paid for his share of beer or pot or gas or food.

Will Wilson was six feet tall then. Lean body, lean face. Dark, seemingly colorless eyes. That day he wore like always a plain t-shirt and jeans. In the winter or in the rain, even working in the cooler at the warehouse on the Tide Flats, Will Wilson wore t-shirts, rarely a flannel shirt or a denim jacket. His straight brown hair touched his shoulder blades like it had since I first met him.

I remember Will Wilson that day at the fair and he seems very handsome.

When the two of us saw kids from Puget Sound and other schools, some of them said *Hey* and some nodded and most of them did recognize us but said nothing. We didn't strut through the crowds like so many of the kids around us. That's not what Will Wilson and I were doing. We were watching. We'd made money that summer. Spent our days and nights on the Tide Flats, apart from anyone else. And now we were back. Kids knew us from parties and from the halls and from our night with Clarence Stark, had heard about break-ins and that we got girls and that we didn't lose fights.

And Will Wilson and I liked that they knew all that. In our lives in Tacoma, those were the things that were important.

We met the two girls at a food stand, Will Wilson from behind them paying for the Cokes and burgers they'd ordered. We sat down with them at an outdoor table. Will Wilson talked much more than me, asking where they went to school, how old they were. He sat with his legs crossed, ankles almost touching. Smiling, staring from one to the other as they spoke. Beth and Julia. Fourteen. Freshman from Lincoln. They looked very much alike, hair long and brown and combed back over their ears, small and soft-looking faces. Both wearing denim coats and jeans, white shirts that had wide, folded collars.

They joked that they weren't here for the rides, they were looking for boys. And when Julia came back from getting a straw, she tapped me on the shoulder and said she wanted to see how tall I was. When I stood, Beth moved to sit next to Will Wilson. Julia reached up to touch the top of my head, then sat down next to me.

Will Wilson started telling them about the cars we'd bought and the money we'd made and how, all summer, we'd worked twelve to sixteen hours a day, leaving work as the sun came up and sitting together with beer in the sunrise.

They liked all that. They looked from him to

me.

The four of us walked around the fairgrounds together and behind the roller coaster they drank from the bourbon.

Julia kept touching me. Every few moments poking me, tapping me, feeling my nylon jacket. Lifting my hand to look closely at the palm.

Behind a row of food stands, there were about twelve small rides. Small fiberglass animals and cars. A small carousel. It was the kiddie zone, with little children riding and waving to their parents. Parents with strollers, parents carrying bags full of prizes. Kids holding large pink elephants, helium balloons tied to their wrists.

Will Wilson asked if these girls wanted to smoke pot and they smiled at each other and nodded.

We found a row of six white, nearly train-car-sized containers behind the kiddie zone. There were a few piles of heavy moving blankets and we sat and smoked the joint.

Julia started kissing me.

And in a few minutes, maybe it was half an hour, Julia was under me, her shirt open under her jean jacket, me opening the front clip of her small bra and rubbing my hand along there and all that, the opening and touching, she'd liked that and wanted that and helped me undo her bra and was kissing me hard with her tongue. I touched her breasts and was even pulling my shirt from my jeans, and she had her hands on my back and it wasn't till I was pushing on her jeans, after I'd unbuckled her belt and was pulling at the top button of her jeans that she said no real weakly and quietly and she was smiling and shaking her head slightly. But I pushed on against her jeans and had the buttons open and was touching her smooth panties, even had my hand on the soft skin of her thigh before she said no again, no between kisses and no while she rubbed her hand over the front of my jeans and against it and seemed to draw its outline against the denim. I could hear the sounds of the fair, the pop guns from the kiddie games and the fast lullaby music from the kiddie carousel and my face around my mouth was wet from her kissing me and kissing me with her tongue, almost licking me with the tip, and when I'd pushed her jeans down to her knees and was rubbing on the outside of her white panties she was saying no and I looked over at Will Wilson on the moving pads a few feet away and he had this girl Beth's jeans off and his jeans were open and I could see her breasts near his mouth and could see her smiling and see Will Wilson's stiff and pink penis above her thighs and I could hear her high voice saying with more air than force, *Right, right,* and he'd pulled her panties down to her ankles and was on her and then pushing his hips against her. And I pulled Beth's panties down to her knees too and was touching my fingers against the inside of her thighs, feeling her wet and gliding and her hands were in my hair, around my ears and pulling at my face, the crash and howl of the roller coaster passing above us in the cool afternoon breeze, and I'd unzipped my jeans and it was a minute before I got myself untangled from my underwear and then I was on top of her and had pressed against the rough hair at her thighs and Julia was shaking her head and saying, *Not yet, no, not now,* and I could feel my zipper against the side of me, my arms around her, all her layers of shirt and bra and denim, and I could feel my coat and my shirt around me and my feet caught up in the clump of shoes and jeans and underwear at her ankles and it was awkward to get my arm down to myself and move the zipper away and help guide myself inside her and then it was dark and thick and easy, so easy, and I glanced at Will Wilson long enough to see that as he pushed against Beth just a few feet away, Will Wilson was watching me, smiling and sucking breaths, and Julia and me were taking sharp breaths too, Julia smiling and holding my face.

We took their phone numbers and they left, saying they had to go catch their ride home. We'd been standing near the entrance to the kiddie zone, all of us smiling awkwardly, except Will Wilson, who smiled some and even kissed Beth out there in the open, which I would never have been able to do.

I was seventeen but had never had a girl-friend.

The sun was just beginning to set. The sky had turned deep blue, thin white clouds grazing the horizon past the roller coaster. Hands went up from the car at the top of the roller coaster's first hill, slow silhouettes of arms and heads and hair.

Will Wilson and I stood next to each other in the center of a small, grassy area. Besides the grass in the center of the horse track, it was the only green I knew of in the Puyallup fairgrounds.

"That girl Julia," Will Wilson said, and paused as he drank from his Coke and bourbon. He spoke again, ice cubes in his mouth. "That was great."

I nodded, seeing him from the corner of my eyes.

"I talked to Linda last night," Will Wilson said.

Linda was a girl from the Tide Flats. She was nineteen and out of high school and she used to sit around in the parking lot with us drinking beer after work.

"She had her abortion yesterday," Will Wilson said.

I turned to him. I hadn't known Linda was pregnant. Will Wilson had spent a lot of time with her that summer and hadn't talked hardly at all about sex with her. For the first time, he was private about that.

I stared at Will Wilson and he watched the roller coaster.

"It was bad," Will Wilson said, then took a drink. Slivers of ice floated on his tongue as he spoke. "I mean," he said, "she was almost going to have it. I gave her the cash. I even wrote her this long letter."

I thought about the girl I'd just had sex with. Came inside. Maybe, I thought, she was on the pill.

"She had to go to Canada and get it done," Will Wilson said. "It cost a lot. She was fucking almost going to have it."

A car on the roller coaster peaked, turned, fell down the first drop, the people all screaming, happy, scared in the cool air.

"My mom was seventeen when she had me," Will Wilson said. "Fuck, she regrets that I'll bet. She got married after I was born and divorced when I turned two and remarried a few years later."

I didn't know what to say. "She's probably glad she had you," I said quietly. And I jerked my head toward him then. Realized. Realized it was the voice I sometimes spoke to Teddy with. Realized it was the voice I had with Kyle.

Will Wilson was already turned to me, face so hard, eyes narrow and bright, leaning forward, moving slowly forward. "Fuck you, don't give me that sympathy shit. Fuck, Porter. How old was your mom when she had you? Boy that was the happiest day of her fucking life. So happy she went on vacation for what is it now, seventeen years? Our moms were afraid of abortion. But I'm sure they wished they could have taken care of us with a fucking coat hanger."

I wanted to step back because I thought he might hit me. But I didn't move.

And Will Wilson, he only turned to the roller coaster, not saying anything more. Leaning his head back as he finished his drink. In a minute, spitting a mouthful of ice onto the grass.

It seems like there was no time to think. Like always, we were already moving. Just ten minutes later, the two of us walking near the games on our way to the parking lot to meet Teddy and Coe, and a big guy in a Lincoln High letterman's jacket bumped hard into Will Wilson's shoulder. The guy was six-six and wide and thick, the coat across his chest covered with pins and patches from the sports he played, his name, Rick, in yellow stitching. He was walking with two friends in matching jackets, though theirs didn't have as many pins or patches and they were no taller than me or Will Wilson.

And Will Wilson would have walked on despite the hard bump from this guy. He hated that stuff, that macho posturing, the tough guy effects. Guys who walked through the fairgrounds or the Tacoma Mall and threw shoulders, turning to say, *What are you going to do, huh? Huh?*

Will Wilson thought that was just silly.

And this Rick was doing it now, saying, "What are you looking at, what are you looking at? Hey, fuck you then."

Will Wilson just smiled some and didn't say anything and stared at Rick. I think that's what got this Rick mad, that Will Wilson didn't go into the standard exchange, didn't challenge or swear or even respond. And so Rick started saying, "So? Huh? So?" and Will Wilson didn't say a word and then this Rick shoved Will Wilson in the shoulder and moved close to shove again. Will Wilson stepped away, turning slowly with the motion of the push but then moving faster, faster as he whirled back to Rick and I heard Rick saying, *Oh, oh,* and Will Wilson hit Rick in the face. And Will Wilson did not stop, did not posture, did not try to be cool or tough. Will Wilson didn't say another word.

The kid's nose had popped on the first hit. A loud, sharp crack.

I didn't see all of what Will Wilson did because when he hit this Rick and Rick stumbled, I turned to Rick's two friends. They'd stepped back, stunned that Will Wilson hadn't gone by the rules. But I knew the friends would try at least to grab Will Wilson. And so I shoved one of them hard enough that he fell and I turned and started hitting the other one in the face. I hit him twice and he was on his knees when the other friend got back up and I turned to him and hit him in the mouth and then the ear and when he fell to the concrete I kicked him in the chest, then in the stomach.

I had glimpses of Will Wilson. But what I know of how he hurt that Rick, I mostly got from some kid at Puget Sound High who sat in the lunch-room a few days later telling his friends about the fight he'd seen, talking quickly as I listened from behind the corner of a vending machine. *First Will Wilson hit this big guy like three times,* the kid told his friends, *and the big guy fell and was holding his face with one hand and half swinging with the other. Will Wilson didn't blink and he waited just a second between punches, taking like a second to aim, hitting this guy above and below the eye, in the ear, in the side of the ribs and then again in the other ear. The big guy was down and looking bad now, this kid was saying, and the other two friends, they hadn't started the fight, but they were getting killed by Brian Porter. Brian Porter was moving more than Will Wilson, circling some, but he was real fucking quiet. Real fucking careful. Will Wilson, though, he was moving so slow, hitting the big kid under the eye as the kid just seemed to struggle to balance on all fours. And then Will Wilson kicked him in the ribs and took the back of the kid's head and smashed his face down, fucking smashed it on the fucking concrete fucking three times hard. Will Wilson not smiling or screaming. That long hair hanging over his eyes and past his shoulders, and fucking still he was hitting this kid. I mean there were two medics there when it was over. Really. For the big kid. I got close to the medics and I heard them say the guy had broken ribs and a broken nose and that his palate, the goddamned fucking roof of his mouth, was broken. The cops came and they asked everyone who'd done it. People gave these descriptions but no one had a name. They asked me and I fucking shrugged. No way. No fucking way. And you know, I remember this from the fight now. I remember how quiet it was. Everyone. The kids getting beaten and the people watching and Brian Porter and Will Wilson especially. You'd think they'd have been screaming or yelling or swearing. But they weren't. They were quiet and it's like it spread, to everyone around them. And I remember this too. I remember how Will Wilson never seemed to look for the other ones, the big kid's friends. It's like he knew they wouldn't get him. Or like he knew Brian Porter would step up and take them out. They never said a word to each other, Brian Porter and Will Wilson. It didn't even seem like they were gonna fight, because Brian Porter and Will Wilson didn't say anything when the big guy was yelling, even when Will Wilson had been shoved. But Will*

Wilson started hitting and Brian Porter started in on these others. Will Wilson just knew he was covered. He knew Brian Porter would help. And fuck. Fuck. I don't know what would have happened, the Puget Sound kid was saying and I stood behind him now, smiling slightly because I'd stepped away from the vending machine and this kid's friends could see me and they were watching me not their friend and it was funny to put some fear into them. *I don't know what would have happened,* the kid went on, *if they'd all been there. If Ted Selva had showed up. Or fuck, fucking Michael Coe.*

We never did talk to Julia or Beth again.

Will Wilson and I met up with Coe and Teddy at the car and as we drove they talked about how they'd split up at some point. Coe had spent the day on every ride he could. The Zipper and The Rotor about four times each, the roller coaster seven. Teddy had gone alone to see The Beach Boys. He'd bought himself a front row seat and a t-shirt and a program. He was so happy he couldn't stop talking about it.

After we'd driven along the river for twenty minutes, Will Wilson started talking very quietly about the fight, and Coe and Teddy didn't talk anymore.

And me, as Will Wilson drove us back to Tacoma, I just listened to him, not talking, sometimes looking at my swollen hands, at the two fingers that would turn out to be broken, replaying the fight as I tried not to think about Julia from the fair, or Linda from the Tide Flats. Or about Will Wilson's mother, or mine.

3   DRIVING AWAY

Sunlight again today, and bright white clouds in the sky. Twelve hundred miles into the drive. Twelve hundred miles from Tacoma.

We drive for a few hours, quiet, and finally I have to pull over in an empty rest stop and sleep a few hours, in the front seat, too tired from the drinking the night before, back in Rawlins. And from the night before that, down at the huts. I sleep in the front seat and it's a dreamless sleep, for three hours removed, blank, gone. I wake up and it's as if I haven't moved or breathed or been here at all.

Kyle is staring at me. He's leaning forward in his seat. His body turned halfway to face me. The rest stop is empty outside the car and I can't even see any cars on the highway. We are very much alone. Which makes it more uncomfortable that he's turned to me, staring.

"How come we didn't go camping?" Kyle asks.

I'm still thinking of being asleep. All of it so blank. Kyle's question seems hard to understand.

"It'd have been much closer," he says. "To go camping."

He seems very still.

I try to wet my lips. "I think we wanted to go on a road trip," I finally say. I have to listen to the words I've spoken. Then listen, first, to what I'm about to say. "We always wanted to go on a road trip."

He's just so very still.

"But when you meet her," he asks, "where will that be?"

Maybe I slept more than three hours.

I say, "It'd have been good to go camping at the Cispus again."

He stares at me. "They flooded that whole valley," he says. "And built a dam."

I nod.

"You know that," he says.

I nod.

"So we couldn't have done that," he says.

"I know," I say.

I've closed my eyes. Tight. Bright outside, so my eyes are closed tight.

"But you forgot," I hear him say.

"I know," I say.

I have to admit that none of it really sounds like Kyle's voice.

"Where will you meet her?" I hear him say.

I'd already forgotten that he'd asked that.

"What does she want?" I hear him say.

I'd already forgotten where she was coming from.

"What do you think you'll say to her?"

I'd already forgotten what she looked like.

"What are you afraid she'll do?"

I'd already forgotten her name.

3   RETURNING

She remembers her brother telling her stories, when she was a little girl. Remembers how they'd hide under her covers, him with his flashlight, telling her about the battles among people they couldn't see. How the people would move through bushes outside the windows, cross the roof in pairs, one then another running quietly then leaping down to the yard outside. And she would hear them after her brother fell asleep, there in her bed, at night, when she couldn't sleep. Her dad didn't own a TV or radio. He'd come home, he'd sit, he'd finally fall asleep. It was a house of total silence, and so what she heard she could hear so clearly, first their steps and the movements, and in the morning her brother would say, *Yes, yes, that's what I mean, don't you see?*

It was all dreaming, really. She'd wake up, in the night or in the morning, and know it was all dreaming. Her brother's crazy fears infecting her as she slept.

And he really was crazy. It's sad. But it would turn out that he wasn't well.

But in the dreams it was real. As real for her as for him. She saw white eyes at her window, staring in on her lying still in her bed. Dark and thick and wet in the dim light, hand on the window, pushing at it without sound. More voices, more faces in the window going wide-eyed, mouths open, teeth caught in the streetlight, screaming now, all the screaming, and in the next moment they were all of them gone.

And she lay there, wet with sweat and pee all across her body, and her own breath covering her face.

And she lay there, shaking, breathing without sound, finding a new silence, a deeper one, the total absence of sound.

Yes, he'd say, her brother, waking up in the morning or waking up when she'd pee, staring at her from just a few inches away. He was her twin and but she never thought she looked like him. *You see? That's what I mean.*

Her brother wasn't well. He'd tell her these things, and as kids she'd believe him. Only later did she realize he wasn't well.

But what matters most, now, is that she is dying. She knows this is true. Just as she knows the dreams aren't real. Knows they only seemed that way.

Her brother's dead too. But that happened years ago. Her father's alive still, but that doesn't matter much. He's got a different house, in a new city, and it's less quiet than the other houses, but she doesn't go there.

The dreams weren't true. But they are back. And maybe they've come back now, returning from childhood, in some effort to give her a distraction. Relief. A childhood memory. Something distant and done.

Or maybe it's just that she's so scared now, about what will happen.

And she stands, and dresses them both, and in ten minutes she is driving the car.

4 NOW
WITH KYLE
TACOMA
DRIVING AWAY
RETURNING

4   NOW

At night, I dream about tunnels so narrow I can barely fit through them. I dream about driving a car faster than I can see. I dream I am in a place so quiet and bright and still. I dream I can fly, lifting as I concentrate on moving myself toward the branches of the trees above me.

I wonder, sometimes, if I've slept at all.

I wonder, sometimes, if I've woken up yet.

And the dreams, they are pretty much always the same.

There was something so sad about Tacoma. Something I couldn't quite see then, or touch, or feel. But that is always there.

I do wake up, though, and there will be children in the bed with us, their bears and tigers and blankets held loose in their hands as they sleep with mouths open, curled up near our pillows, or my daughter who always makes a nest on the floor, near my side of the bed, never crawling in with us, but nesting close, near me, and I know their dreams have been worse than mine, simple fears about falling or monsters or losing that bear, simple fears that are worse than mine, it's not about my fears, my dreams, or me, and I'm awake now and I see them all and I know they will be fine, another day, another day, work hard, do well for them, make it all be fine.

4   WITH KYLE

I stood near the stern with Kyle and the crew, barely listening to the priest in front of us, only watching the sunset in his eyes. The priest was a short man and he stood alone on the large hatch cover as he spoke, the pages of the Bible in his hands, yellow in the sunlight, his glasses flashing bright with gold.

"They went out and got into the boat," I heard him saying, *"but that night they caught nothing."*

I took a drink from my plastic cup of beer. For a second, with my eyes closed, I could feel the boat pulling at the dock, stretching on the ropes, then releasing.

This was the boat blessing. The crew, mostly Kyle's cousins and uncles, were leaving for Alaska early the next morning.

I took a drink and looked over my shoulder. Across the narrow waterway, up the hill between the buildings of downtown Tacoma, was the sun. I squinted behind my sunglasses and could see its shape, a wavering disk in a sky turned very blue, and for a second I could see the close reflection of my face and eyes caught in the lenses.

"Just as the day was breaking, Jesus stood on the beach, yet the disciples did not know it was Jesus."

Downtown Tacoma was very dark, the bare streets, the few parked cars, the low buildings all in shadows. I could hear one car driving. Just one. Couldn't see it but could hear the engine rising and falling as it accelerated.

I turned slowly back toward this priest, seeing down the waterway the smokestacks of the pulp mill. I could see Skinny's, a bar where the crew drank and where a few times I'd gone with Kyle, sitting with the crew as they talked about going to Alaska. I could see the fishing boats tied up in the small marina around us. And it was all very still, I was thinking. The city, the water, the forty people around us on the boat and standing next to us on the dock. Everything seemed like it was waiting. Friday afternoon in that lull before the weekend starts. A day before the boat left. Friday afternoon, a week before we'd graduate. A week before Kyle was leaving to work at a fish plant in Alaska.

Maybe everything was always waiting. Maybe I just didn't look around real often and see it. But drinking with a priest makes you think, maybe. You slow down for a second. You look around. You think.

"'Children, have you any fish?'"

I looked around as the priest spoke, trying to see if Kyle's oldest uncle was there. The old man had never been real big on these things. Even for the blessings of his own boat, he'd just stay for the prayer, usually leave quick after the priest was done and the party was really starting. Now, sick like he was, real thin and distracted, the old man probably hadn't come. But maybe he'd show up later, I was thinking. Just to give Kyle a new pocket knife even.

Like always. Handing it off and nodding and not saying much.

Maybe the old man would come just to say good-bye.

I felt the Saint Christopher medal in my pocket. Smooth against my hand. The old man had given it to me that week. He'd given it to Kyle to give to me and I hadn't worn it, but I'd kept it in my pocket. It was from the old man. Kyle's dad's brother. It seemed like I should hang on to it.

Just that past winter, the old man had had a stroke. He couldn't fish now. He couldn't talk too well and he was walking with a cane.

He was going to die real soon. Anybody could see it.

I looked over at the fishing boat docked in the slip next to us. It was the old man's boat, a seventy foot seiner like the one we were on, freshly painted by Kyle and his cousins, tied up and ready to just lie in the slip for the summer. "I've painted it every year," the old man had said. "Let's just paint the damn thing."

"And bless them. And bless them. And bless them. And bless them."

This priest's voice was uneven and slow and comfortable. I'd never seen him before but it seemed like that was probably always his way.

I looked down and saw Kyle was pouring bourbon into my beer.

I took a drink from the beer and whiskey. It made my eyes water a bit, made the boat and this priest and these people standing around us all seem brighter in the sunset. They were Slavs mostly. Dark hair, dark eyes. Family to Kyle, most of them people who fished or who were married to fishermen or who were the sons and daughters of fishermen.

I'd been friends with Kyle since we were six years old, but it wasn't till this spring that I'd thought about him being Slavic. That I thought about him being any different than me. But he was. His grandfather had come from Slovenia to California. Kyle's mom and uncles and cousins all went to gatherings of other Slavic families a few times a year. They married Slavs and had Slavs work on their boats.

I wasn't Slavic or Catholic. I didn't have a family who went to blessings. They didn't even get together for Christmas.

"And Jesus said to them, 'Set the net on the star*board side of the boat, and you will find some.' So they cast it, and now they were not able to haul it in, for the quantity of fish."*

"Set on the starboard side," Kyle said quietly and tapped his cup against mine.

And then this priest asked the crew to come up onto the hatch. "Set on the starboard side," Kyle said loudly as the crew stepped up and Kyle raised his cup to the people around us.

People laughed and the priest and Kyle both smiled.

And I was surprised that Kyle could joke about what that priest had said. To me, what that priest said was untouchable, what he did somehow unmentionable. I had never touched a Bible. I had never been inside a church. There'd just never been any reason.

I saw Kyle had his head down and had taken off his sunglasses.

"For the people who have not come back," the priest was saying. *"Think of them."*

The boat was very quiet and I had my head down and taken my glasses off and I wanted to set down my drink but there was nowhere to put it.

"And bless them. And bless them. And bless them. And bless them."

Kyle, a week earlier, had told me he'd gotten me a job at a fish plant with him, up on the Kenai Peninsula in Alaska. We'd leave in a few days.

We'd talked about Alaska, about work up there, for years. Now it was here. He'd taken care of everything. But I wasn't sure how I could go. Wasn't sure how to leave.

I didn't know what Will Wilson would say.

"And bless them. And bless them. And bless them. And bless them."

It was later, and I was staring down, seeing the water catching corners of light in the small waves, ridges running aimlessly behind and beneath me.

The sky was orange and red and almost night.

Kyle and I were sitting up on the wheelhouse.

The people on the deck below us were putting food in their mouths, then beer or water or scotch. Smiling with their food, with their drinks. The priest still in the middle of it all, still standing on the hatch cover, the Bible near his chest.

I said after a minute, "I'll be glad to be on the

way."

I said after another minute, "I wonder what kind of prices we'll get."

Kyle pushed his lips together, blinking as he slowly said, "They'll be good enough. I don't even really care so much about the money anymore. Just to be going. That's what I think about." He leaned his head back. "I'm pretty drunk already," he said.

There's always a reason for that priest, I was thinking. Always an excuse.

"You got a lot of family here," I said.

Kyle's eyes had closed and his head was leaning back even farther.

So much family, I was thinking. Cousins and aunts and all of them together on this boat.

On the deck above the party, Kyle was asleep, his head back, mouth open.

We sat that way for about twenty minutes, Kyle sleeping and me quiet, looking down at the party. *How do I tell him I can't go?*

Kyle jerked forward and was awake. He looked around, at me and down at the people. Up at the sky.

"I feel better," he said.

Kyle could do that. Sleep for a few minutes and wake up feeling like he'd slept for an hour.

He was looking toward the few lit windows in Tacoma's downtown buildings. "You remember at your house when we were kids and we'd make popcorn," Kyle was saying, "and how we'd just cover your living room floor with it? Throw it in the air and try to catch it in our mouths but always miss. Trying to miss because it was so funny to cover that floor with popcorn. I think I just dreamt about that."

I looked down toward the people. Lifted my cup from near my feet. Took a long drink. In a moment, I said, "Yes."

Kyle was looking at me in a way that made me sort of nervous, in a way I wasn't used to.

"You're coming to Alaska, right?" he said.

I nodded.

Kyle stood up. "It's a good place to start, a fish plant," he said. Kyle stretched and rubbed his hand across his mouth. "In the fall, after working there, we can get on a boat, like this one." He was moving toward the ladder with his cup in his hand. "These people, most of them, they're very happy. And if you think about it, you don't find a lot of people who are happy."

And I only drank again, emptying my cup.

It was later, and I could barely see the people beyond the shine above me, silhouettes moving and even dancing on the hatch and near the rails. People on the dock talking and drinking, their voices howling high and empty down the quiet waterway.

Two hours into the party. The boat's lights on. Extra cords of bulbs strung up and around.

I was pushing a hand across my face, feeling my cheeks and nose all numb and distant, drinking and swallowing and feeling that drink already through my neck to my chest. Swallowing slowly, the drink warm through my mouth. Swallowing slowly and holding a piece of ice near my throat.

"There is no blessing," I started saying to Kyle, my mouth moving thickly and carefully, lips spreading with words, tongue dragging across sounds. "There's no fucking prayer on this boat and no fucking Christ on this boat. No fucking Jesus looking over us."

Kyle was smiling. Kyle was smiling wide and drunk and he was nodding. "I don't think so," he said. "I don't. But it's not so bad like that. Not so empty like you say."

There were bare bulb lights shining bright in my face, all so close and hanging from a cord, swinging slow with that all but unnoticed motion of a boat in a slip.

"Oh it's fucking empty," I was saying loudly, pouring more vodka into my cup, dropping ice in after it. "It's fucking empty."

"It's just family," Kyle said, smiling and drinking, his voice fading then growing as he spun slowly in place. "It's family together and thinking of one thing. Thinking together. That's all a blessing is. For me. Maybe for that priest it's more. Maybe for him it's about Christ looking down on us." Kyle laughed, holding his cup out and grinning. "I guess for him it would have to be more. I mean, that's what he's paid for."

I poured his cup full of vodka. Gave him only one chunk of ice. "Drink and get drunk," I said.

"Drink and get drunk," Kyle repeated, smiling still as he raised his cup to me.

"Fucking lights," I said, stepping away from the bulbs above me. Kyle was getting hugged by some huge man in a tightly fitting suit. The man hugged and hugged. Lifting Kyle. Squeezing him hard.

Kyle just smiled. Trying to take a drink. Face turning red from the pressure.

Kyle's mom was hugging Kyle now. Shaking his head. He just nodded. Smiled. Tried when he could to take a gulp from his drink. Even in the dim light, his face looked nearly purple.

Kyle hadn't lived with his mom for years. But he smiled and kissed her on the cheek. I could see she was drunker than anyone on that boat. I could see her brother, one of Kyle's uncles, standing behind her, keys in his hand, ready to take her home.

And I turned to look down the waterway, drank and swallowed and saw him then. On his boat. Next to us. Sitting on the deck. Staring at the party, I thought. Kyle's uncle. The old man. Cane in his hand. Staring up at his boat, I realized. Not looking at the party. Turned to his cabin and wheelhouse. The boom and lines. The wheel up top. There in the dark, sitting, just staring.

"Jesus is your captain," a voice said near my ear.

I turned and there was the priest, dark head bowed forward, looking at me over his glasses.

I could only nod. Lower the cup from my lips. "Yes," I said. "Sure."

The priest was smiling some. "It is a joke, young man," he said, his teeth showing small and tight.

I nodded, not sure what he meant.

"Jesus is your captain," the priest said again. "I say that to joke."

I nodded, smiling. Trying to find a way to laugh.

"Good luck," he said, touching my shoulder. "Be safe."

"Oh, no," I said. "I'm not on the crew."

He nodded. "I know," he said. "But you're going with Kyle. Up to Alaska. Be safe there too."

I nodded, nodding, nodding because I couldn't speak to him. Thought anything I'd say would be wrong, anything I did bad.

"It's a good thing that Kyle's doing," the priest said.

I nodded, not sure what he meant.

"Stay with him," he said. "And you will be fine."

I only nodded.

"It is words and wishes and thoughts," he said then and I didn't know what he meant. "This blessing is not to you what it is to me. But, Brian," he said, leaning close, smiling some again as his glasses caught the light from the bulbs, "it's not so empty. Not so fucking empty at all."

And as he walked away I turned to the old man's boat, drinking from my cup, swallowing hard. But the old man was gone. And down the dock, beyond the lights from our boat, there was someone standing. Thin and still and watching me. And I was drunk, so drunk, but I was sure it was Will Wilson. Watching. Watching everything.

I woke up very early in the morning needing

water. I was in a bunk on the boat and I had my jeans on still and I didn't remember going to sleep.

Kyle was in the bunk across from me, his mouth open, his hand swinging down over the edge of the bunk.

My head hurt and my body hurt and right then, like that, it was hard to feel bad about anything else. I could think about things, but I couldn't think about them as good or think about them as bad. My knees ached, my chest hurt. I felt that.

I didn't know if I should go. To Alaska with Kyle. Didn't know how. How to leave.

I climbed the steps to the bright and cold galley. I drank water with my arms pressed across my chest. Slowly slid my bare foot back and forth across the cold linoleum floor.

I drank more water and the galley got brighter with the sun coming up and after a few minutes I turned and saw someone outside near the stern. There was dew on the window and I didn't know who it was. For a second I was afraid, suddenly, but I went outside anyway, and the air was much colder, the deck wet against my feet, but the cold feeling good against my face and neck.

The old man was bent over slightly, coiling a rope that lay on the deck. His thick hands moved very slowly, carefully untwisting the line, laying the coils even and flat. I saw his cane against the net pile.

"Good morning," I said after he had finished.

"Oh, yeah," the old man said and turned toward me. "Who's that," he said, creased face twisting some as he looked in my direction. His vision had gotten real bad since the stroke. "Oh, yeah. Yeah," he said when I'd stepped closer. "Morning," he said.

There was something so distant about the old man. The way he talked in these sudden bursts of sound, the way he never looked at you for too long. But it was kind of nice. Part of the old man was always somewhere else, doing something better.

"Leaving soon," he said.

"Yeah. I think they're leaving around noon."

He was nodding and looking over at his boat.

I looked toward downtown, saw it more still now than the night before.

I looked down at my feet. They had turned pink.

"Good," said the old man but I didn't know what he meant. "Have you got your Saint Christopher?" he asked.

"Yeah," I said and took it from my pocket. I looked at it and I thought the old man was watching me. I slipped the chain over my head.

I looked up and saw he was staring at his boat.

"A Saint Chris is good luck," he said.

"What are you going to do with yourself this summer," I said and then felt stupid.

The old man reached into his pocket. "Here," he said. He handed me two pocket knives.

"Thanks," I said quietly.

He was nodding.

"Was getting one for Kyle and all," he said.

The old man nodded.

"I didn't think Kyle should wait," said the old man. "But I guess it's right. He'll be on the boat in the fall."

I wasn't sure what he meant.

"I'm glad he's helping you, though," the old man said. "Work hard, and he'll get you on the boat. It's all right for him to wait."

The old man picked up his cane and looked at it absently.

I had my head down to look at the knife and the Saint Christopher was small and warm against my chest and I felt the old man moving toward me, looking at me.

I'd realized Kyle was supposed to be on this boat, be a part of this crew. He was waiting, though, going to Alaska with me instead.

"Wear that Saint Chris," the old man said. "Work hard," he said. "Work hard. Work hard."

I'd forgotten about seeing Will Wilson the night before. I only remembered that much later.

One of those same small houses with the garages out back, the garages we'd burned, a house like that had been built on Thirtieth Street, an Old Town hill overlooking the bay. The houses in that neighborhood were much larger and nicer than the rest of Tacoma and more attention had been given to the painting of them and to the landscaping of the yards. But, like so many of those small, box-like Tacoma homes, this house stood isolated on its piece of property, no shrubs, no fence. This one didn't even have a garage.

The house was going to be demolished soon. It was late February, when we were eighteen, a few months before we graduated. And after she moved out, but before the house was torn down, the woman who owned it told her son he could have some people over. They could write on the walls, put a few holes in the doors. The mother had said she didn't care. She was getting city money no matter what, because a park behind the property was going to be extended.

The kid threw a very big party.

When the four of us got there, the house was full of people, music was playing on a portable box. The kid had told everyone that the electricity would be off, so most people had brought flashlights and candles and camping lights. The bare walls were lit yellow in some rooms, a barren white in others. In some, there were only the faintest shadows of people talking and drinking in the smoke.

People had knocked small holes in the walls, spray-painted names and messages on doors and windows.

Home of the Rams
Go Air Force
The bottomless pit

We talked to some people at the party, but this was after Clarence Stark, after the garage burnings, and after years of fights. And so the four of us really stood slightly aside, so tightly bound to each other, so separate from everyone else. And these other kids, some of them didn't want to talk to us or wanted to but thought that they couldn't. And I know that a lot of them were afraid of us.

I remember Jodi Robart was there and Will Wilson said hi to her and she smiled a little and nodded. She wasn't living at his house then. She'd been living with a friend's family for a few years.

I remember how there were a couple of other girls there that I'd had sex with or that some of the other three had had sex with. We saw them and some we smiled at or even talked to. A couple barely smiled. A couple more wouldn't look at us, just seemed to move themselves deeper into the crowd.

There was still beer in the keg, and the worst thing was that Coe was already drunk when we got there. He couldn't quite raise his head to eye level, his stringy hair hanging over his eyes and nose. He drank two more beers in his first ten minutes in the house and kids were already giving him room to stumble in place and then he put an ax through a door, couldn't get it out and so he tore the door off the hinges with his hands.

It wasn't so much that Coe was angry. He'd just gotten excited about the idea of openly damaging this house. And so, under the Proctor Bridge, where we'd been before the party, Coe drank too much.

The three of us now took Coe to the basement, away from anyone else. There, in the dim, shifting light of two candles, we watched Coe tear heating ducts off the ceiling, rip a door off a storage area. We watched Coe turn to the set of wooden stairs we'd come down, breaking off the steps, throwing each one hard in our direction, the three of us having to sidestep and duck. Coe tore off the hand rail and in the dark basement he tried to joust with Teddy, Teddy laughing hard, easily stepping aside, a few times running Coe head-on into the poles that supported the stairs. Kids were standing at the open doorway above us and when Coe saw them through the hair over his eyes, he threw pieces of wood at them, finally tearing down what was left of the stairs, the heavy wood crashing loudly, echoing through the concrete room.

Coe started yelling, "Let's burn this place down." His voice was heavy, his thick chest heaving. "Fuck Will, right? We're going to burn this place down, right?"

Will Wilson smiled and carefully grabbed

Coe's shoulders. He turned Coe back to where the stairs had been. "No, no," he said. "No, no. And besides, how would we get out of here?"

Teddy was laughing, standing behind Coe and lightly touching Coe's ears so that Coe twitched his head. "We'll burn in hell," Teddy whispered.

Coe swung around, looking for another way out. Most of the homes like this had a door that led from the basement to the backyard. But this one didn't. It took Coe a few minutes to realize the doorway had been covered. Two six-by-nine pieces of drywall had been put up, the only drywall on the basement's concrete walls.

Coe ran at the pieces with a board from the stairs, hammering away, the drywall breaking. The board fell from his hands and he began tearing at the drywall, kicking and punching, chalky dust floating in the dim basement light. Coe tore and punched, reached plywood and was now kicking at that. The three of us stood drinking beer behind him. Coe hadn't turned around, just fought the wall, and in a few minutes cool air from the outside poured into the basement, the candles flickering as Coe threw his body at the plywood, two times crashing against it before flying through to the old concrete steps that led up to the backyard. He collapsed on the lawn, face and hair white with chalk, his eyes and mouth seeming very black.

Will Wilson and I sat down on an old barrel on the lawn. Teddy went around to the front of the house to get us more beer. I asked Will Wilson if he wanted to go back into the party. He shook his head.

"So," I said, taking a last drink of beer, watching Coe's unmoving, clown-like white face in front of us. "What now?"

"Fuck, Porter," Will Wilson said quietly, "we're going to burn this place down."

We did wait until everyone had left. Will Wilson, Teddy and I carried Coe through the shadows behind the house to the big swing set in the park next door, hid him in a steel tube that during the day kids climbed through for fun. We moved our car to a parking lot a few blocks away. And then we came back to the park, drinking and watching from about fifty yards away as people left the party.

Around two o'clock in the morning, the three of us quietly went back to the house with a liter bottle full of gas from Will Wilson's car and climbed inside through the basement hole Coe had opened. Teddy and I boosted Will Wilson up to the door where the stairs had started. He was making sure no one was in the house.

"Shit," Teddy whispered to me in the dark. "Shit. This is serious. This is a fucking house. Fuck, Brian, fuck. This is serious, Brian."

"It's going to be demolished anyway," I whispered. "There were all those candles here. People will think it was one of the candles."

"People will know it was us," Teddy whispered. "They saw Coe going wild. They probably heard him say that we wanted to burn it down."

"Well," I said. "Fuck. Well."

Will Wilson dropped down next to us with

matches and a camp light someone had forgotten.

There were paint cans and a nearly full can of paint thinner in the storage room. There was also a lawn chair, an old croquet set and a cardboard box full of books. We spread out the junk and books and some boards from the stairs, then poured thinner and gas over it all, set the unlit camp light in the middle of it.

Will Wilson was holding a book of matches out to Teddy and me, but not looking at us. We were all near the hole to the backyard and Will Wilson lit a match and tossed it, then another, the gas catching. Teddy kept looking over his shoulder, glancing up into the backyard.

"Come on," Will Wilson said, still not looking at Teddy and me, just flicking matches across the floor, small blue fires now burning in four or five places.

And finally I lit a match. Lit it and threw it because Will Wilson wanted me to. But, most of all, I lit it because I wanted to be a part of this. I wanted to burn down a house.

Blue flames had spread across much of the floor. A small pool near the books ignited.

I lit and threw another match.

And Teddy was starting to go out of the hole and Will Wilson turned quickly, grabbed him hard by the neck, pulling Teddy close to his face. "Come on," he said quietly and held up a lit match for Teddy.

The books were burning orange and red, the wood catching now. The plastic seat of the lawn chair burning bright, shining on Will Wilson's face and Teddy's face and sending a foul smell through the room.

"Come on," Will Wilson said, and then smiled and took a high voice. Whining, *"This is serious."*

And Teddy did light a match and did throw it then, lighting another and another, tossing each into the already hot fire, the tiny match disappearing in the gold and growing light, but Teddy just stared at Will Wilson, not scared, not weak, just staring, Will Wilson holding him by the neck and not once looking at the fire behind him, whining over and over, *"This is serious. This is serious. This is serious."*

We watched the fire from the park a hundred yards away, all of us hidden behind a set of slides. The reflection of the flames flickered in the house's window panes, smoke rose in puffs from the doors. In a few minutes, flames reached through the hole in the basement, later broke through the roof. We could hear sirens. Trucks came. We watched the firefighters put out the flames, spraying water for about an hour as neighbors stood in the street.

Will Wilson was smiling. So was Coe, who'd woken up and now sat staring at the fire, face still covered with chalk. Lips so red, eyes so dark.

Teddy stared down at the ground between his knees, every few moments spitting into the dirt.

But I didn't look much at Teddy. I mostly watched those flames. And from there in our darkness by the slides, it did seem like the four of us were nearing something. Money from working in summer, money from after school jobs. Girls in cars. Girls in the gulch. Houses that we still broke into. And now a house that we'd burned down. In that nighttime quiet, I felt like some calm had come, felt like there wasn't much more we could do. And I was, in a way, disappointed.

But, later, I'd look back on burning that house and know it was different. Know that, really, we had only just started. Because, it seems now, everything till then had been only small, simple steps in a still expanding plan.

•

When we were fifteen, we all had cars. We weren't legal yet, but Teddy had his cousin's car and Will Wilson and Coe had given money to their parents to buy them cars. I'd bought a car that I kept at Coe's. And in Tacoma, with a car, you could drive to the good pot dealers near Point Defiance and Old Town and you could drive to the all-night stores near Hilltop that didn't check i.d.'s. With a car you could go to four or five parties in one night, could go by the Puget Sound High parking lot and the old burger place called Frisko Freeze. You could go to the edge of the gulch near Stadium High School and climb down to the huts, drinking beer and looking out at the bay and the Tide Flats and Shuster Parkway below.

And you could do it all in one night.

Will Wilson would drive us to older kids' parties back then, the seniors' parties and the parties of kids who were nineteen and twenty. And if at a party or a parking lot Will Wilson was given shit by some kid, even an older one, Will Wilson just stared, not moving or responding, but staring till the kid got mad, and then he'd push Will Wilson. And then Will Wilson would beat up that kid, sometimes the four of us taking on the kid and his friends. Breaking the mirrors off their cars as they struggled to stand, snapping antennas and kicking out headlights, putting rocks through their windshields.

We were fifteen and we felt good. These things mattered, cars and work that paid you good money, and buying beer or pot easy, and walking into a room and beating up a stranger and his friends, and being a group, each of us multiplied by the presence of the others.

There were girls who wanted to be with us because of this, too. Who wanted to be with us because we had beer and pot. Because we always knew of parties. Because we could give them a ride. These were the girls who raced down Pearl at eighty miles an hour, the girls who got in fights not where they scratched and pulled hair but threw hard punches and wrestled on the concrete. This was Tacoma, my Tacoma, a place of force and violence. A place where the people I knew worked hard, earned money by the hour and wanted to spend it proudly on things, on cars and records and fast food.

Girls would come up to us, especially Will Wilson, at school or at parties. Older girls, younger girls. Not starry-eyed chicks throwing themselves at our feet. But girls who would do the things teen-agers do, every day at school stand by Will Wilson's locker or mine, at parties bump purposely into Ted-dy or me, ask Will Wilson or Teddy to get them beer from the keg. Rarely doing anything to Coe. Coe was too strange, with his lips that were always wet, his pants and shirt hanging loose off his pasty body.

Will Wilson could talk easily or stand just slightly aside, half-smiling and still-faced. And with his dark eyes and long hair and lean face, Will Wilson was good-looking. There were girls who knew nothing about Will Wilson except that he seemed good-looking.

And although the two of us weren't easy with girls, Teddy and I learned from watching Will Wilson that we could say very little, and girls would talk to us.

Some of these girls who wanted to meet us, they had ideas about parking along the waterfront and making out. They would say that sometimes and we would do that sometimes. And some of these girls who got in cars with us and went down to the huts or utility sheds with us, they'd had sex before, were from the start of the night thinking about having sex with one of us.

Most every weekend night we were looking for girls, although we actually talked to girls only once in a while, convinced them to get in the car with us maybe only every few weeks. It sometimes didn't seem like very much.

I can remember some night when we were sixteen, when there were three girls who hesitated about getting in the car, one deciding not to, the two others finally getting in. Two fifteen-year-olds, one in jeans and a black t-shirt and leather jacket, the other in a denim miniskirt and heavy sweater. We drove and drank and they said sure when Will Wilson talked about going down into the gulch. They said yes.

That night Will Wilson parked and they ran past us, leading the way down the darkened trails to the huts, Will Wilson smiling as he called directions to them, left on that trail, climb over that trunk. When the four of us got to the huts, they were sitting next to each other on one of the roofs.

We all drank and Coe made a fire. These girls stayed on the roof and Will Wilson held beers out for them. "Come down and get one," he kept saying. But they wouldn't, just smiled and shook their heads, swung their feet. Then Will Wilson handed the beer up to them.

The fire was shining gold light on Coe's face as he put on more wood. Teddy and I stood near the fire, not talking, looking from the girls to the flames. I can remember the red sparks floating past my face to these girls, remember how they waved them away like fireflies, smiling and talking quietly to each other, staring out at the dark bay.

After almost an hour, they both kicked off their shoes and the one in the miniskirt asked Will Wilson to rub her feet, the one in the leather jacket asked Teddy to rub hers. Teddy and Will Wilson stood below them, Will Wilson pushing slowly against the one girl's skin, staring up at her on the hut. Teddy touching his girl's feet lightly and not looking at her face.

"There's too many people," one girl whispered.

Will Wilson lit a joint and passed it up to them, saying, "Finish it. Go ahead. There's more."

Will Wilson and Teddy were still rubbing these girls' feet and Coe gave them two more beers and in ten minutes Teddy's girl dropped down from the roof, almost falling as she landed.

The other girl wouldn't come down. Five minutes of Will Wilson touching her feet, of the other girl hanging drunkenly on Teddy. But the girl in the miniskirt stayed on the hut, staring out toward the bay, smiling.

And then Will Wilson stopped rubbing, wrapped his hands around her ankles, and began to pull. Lightly. Steadily. She didn't notice till her thighs were past the roof's edge. Will Wilson pulled smiling and she was saying, "Careful. Wait. Careful." And he still pulled, reaching one hand up to her thighs, holding her as she came off the hut, letting her slowly drop. And as she slid down into his arms, her skirt was lifting. Her dark panties showing. Will Wilson's hands just touching them, the girl's bare feet almost reaching the ground.

"Okay," this girl in the miniskirt was saying, smiling, her eyes open wide but her head nodding, drunk. "Okay."

And Will Wilson, he had his face so close to hers in the gold light from the fire, and now he was saying it too, saying, "Okay, okay."

The girl was reaching to her skirt and Will Wilson moved his arms, pulling her closer as if hugging her whole body, carefully holding her in his thin arms.

Will Wilson only smiling and walking with her now, carrying her awkwardly into one of the huts.

"Where are we going?" the other girl was asking.

"All of you," Will Wilson's girl was saying. "All of you."

Coe had gone into another hut alone. I could see his hand sticking out from the darkness, slowly waving at Teddy. And in a minute, Teddy did walk in there, girl smiling, eyes closed, head bobbing. Coe in the dark waiting.

I stood in the doorway of Will Wilson's hut, the light from the fire barely reaching the room. "Now," his girl was saying absently, slurring. "Both of you now." And as my eyes adjusted, I could see he already had her sweater up and her bra open. He was pushing up her skirt and I watched him pull open his jeans.

"There," she said slowly, touching his face. "And you too."

And then he lowered himself onto her and was pushing on her and she was moaning.

I could hear from the other hut the girl saying thickly, "Yes."

After a few minutes, Will Wilson motioned me over and he stood and I unzipped my pants and was leaning down and then was inside her and pushing on her and she was moaning loud, her hands raised to my face, then falling, raising again. Saying, "Please. Please. Both, please."

At the fire afterward I would remember it feeling good. I would remember leading her to what she must have known we were going to do. And thinking that way, and seeing Will Wilson like always smiling at the three of us, then there didn't seem to be any way to feel anything but good. No way to touch that other feeling inside, something hollowed and cold and barren and sorry. Standing by the fire with my three best friends, drinking again, smoking pot with the vodka turning your face so distant and thick, the rest of you numb in the cold air beyond the glow of the fire, for only a moment glancing back, seeing this girl through the doorway, stumbling in the shadows, leaning heavily against a wall as she slowly looked for her panties in the dark.

Girls in cars, in parking lots, in houses I couldn't have ever found again. In the huts and in the dirt of the gulch and drinking and smoking and sharing a joint and a beer and a body, wet, breathing, on a bed on a chair on a seat on the ground in the dirt near a tree till it ended and you're done.

And afterward you'd both have to get dressed. Both of you in your underwear, laying on top of her in the wet leaves, branches pressed against your bare arms, jeans pushed down to your feet. Standing and you'd see her turn away, her back and bottom dirty, this girl dressing quickly while trying to cover herself. Turned slightly away, maybe leaning up against a tree, but watching you carefully from the corners of her eyes.

•

The guy was still smiling as I broke his finger. My hand already holding his thick, wet hair, pulling his head back and another finger back and I was pulling him to the ground, the side of his head smacking loud against the sidewalk, the second finger breaking easily in my hand.

When I was a child, one night I watched my dad lean over the kitchen sink, washing blood from his swollen face as I stood near my babysitter, Amelia. *There's nothing you can't do in a fight, Brian,* he said to me quietly, his voice slowed and heavy. Long hair in his blue eyes. Pushing his fingers along the thin lines leading to his lips. Twenty-two years old. Maybe twenty-three. *You just want to win, Brian. You just want to hurt him.*

I was hitting this guy in the face now, striking his nose, his eye, his cheek. We were in front of a mini-market near school and it was raining, hard, after school and this guy, eighteen, he'd pushed Teddy hard into a door, being cool in front of his friends, this guy from school who'd tried to push Teddy around a few times that week, and today I'd told him to fuck off, and he'd turned to me, smiling, leaning close and pointing his finger in my face, smiling down at me, a foot or more taller because I was younger.

I was still hitting him now, the guy pulling

away, standing and turning to me, hands raised and he swung hard and straight and hit me in the eye and I was against his chest and hit him across the jaw and in the ear and he was falling, my hand catching his long hair again and this time I wrapped my fingers in it, held tight as he fell, hitting him in the ear and neck and I dropped on his spine with my knee, was pulling his head back and his eye was open wide and he was moaning now, reaching his arms out and grabbing my ankle and I hit that open eye three then four times, grabbed his hand from my ankle and broke three fingers at once, bending them back as I stepped on the wrist.

"Fucker," I said quietly, feeling the rain falling lightly on my lips as I spoke. Breathing steadily, finding a rhythm between my words and motions. Feeling all that anger, feeling it run through my chest and arms and hands.

And I turned slightly as I swung, seeing Teddy standing near the window of the store. Watching.

And the guy's friends, they hadn't moved.

The guy rolled away from me, standing and turning and trying to find me, his right eye covered with blood and the left side of his face bleeding too, his twisted hand wiping at his good eye and when he saw me he came at me. Not wildly. Moving forward, saying, "No," and breathing hard. Swinging straight and almost hitting me again. "No."

I hit him in the throat and he leaned over. I moved to my left. Watching him gag. I kicked him in the chest.

The guy was kneeling, leaning. Sucking

breaths. I grabbed his smooth, wet hair. I tilted his head back and hit him three times in the nose, the second shot breaking it with a loud, solid pop. The third landing soft and knocking him to the ground.

"Don't ever," I said. Spitting blood from my lips. Tasting blood in my throat. "Don't ever fuck with my friend."

Teddy had stepped forward. Standing on the curb, a few feet away. Watching.

The guy's nose poured red and yellow blood. He sat up. I knocked him onto his back. Knee in his chest, holding his hard, wet jaw. He was trying to get away, but I held his mouth, aiming with my right fist, waiting. He closed his mouth and I hit him, broke a tooth.

My hands were wet with spit and blood and rain.

I pulled back my arm and fist. The swing started in my chest. I broke another of his teeth, blood and mucus flying toward Teddy.

I was tired. I was mad.

The guy looked toward his friends, three of them standing on the sidewalk. He stared at them for a moment, but didn't ask for help. Didn't expect them to do anything. And they were only watching.

I hit him in the ear. His face hit the street. He was laid out on his side. In a moment, he asked dully, "Why won't you stop?"

I leaned close to him. Whispering. "Don't fuck with my friend."

And the guy was nodding slowly, the side of his head dragging across the street.

I pulled tight against his scalp. Pressed my knee against the side of his face, felt the point of his jaw below his ear.

Will Wilson had showed up. Walking toward me. Stopping near Teddy. Not smiling, just watching. He carefully sat down. Cross-legged on the wet sidewalk. Watching.

"Don't fuck with my friend," I said again, and saw the guy's eyes wide and he was moaning and trying to push me away and my arms were heavy and burning and my chest tight and he lifted his head and I stood as he did and stepped forward and kicked him, in the mouth, the point of my shoe, and he fell back.

I was tired. I was mad.

I turned to look at Will Wilson and, behind him, in the window of the store, I could see my reflection. Hair so wet in the rain. Hair that hung straight past my dark eyes.

The guy was screaming, blood and spit spraying across the street. I covered his mouth with my hands, his teeth against my palm, his tongue against my fingers. I leaned very close, my chest against his, holding him down. "Don't fuck with my friend," I whispered.

I walked to the curb and kneeled at a puddle, rinsing my hands in the cool rainwater. Two fingers on my right hand were numb and bent. I turned my face to the sky, let the rain run down my eyes and neck. Wiped the water away before again rinsing my hands in the puddle. Again wiping at my face before the three of us met up with Coe and we all walked home, fourteen, and right then none of us had a car.

•

Once, in a house, I left Will Wilson in a kitchen as he slowly made his way through every drawer and cabinet, passed Coe in the dining room climbing across a fireplace mantle. I was looking for Teddy and found him in the living room, a wide, tall room with windows open onto the bay and the bright ships and the lights of the neighborhoods all around us, and he was climbing up the windows, in bare feet with his toes just balanced on the thin frames of the windows, fifteen feet in the air now, and he was looking out of a skylight, his hands touching the panes of the glass, his face close to the frame.

"What are you doing?" I whispered, as loud I could.

I could see he was talking, but I couldn't hear him.

"What are you looking for?" I asked again.

We were eighteen. We'd been breaking into houses for so long now. The fighting and the cars and girls in the gulch. There were days when I felt old and tired and worn out by it all.

Teddy was still talking quietly, his fingers running along the edges of the skylight, his head turned upward, and I thought I heard more the echo of his voice, coming back to me off that window, and I've never known if he knew I was there.

"Something pretty," Teddy whispered, "something beautiful."

•

Walter Mitchell was a very smart kid from my high school who played a lot of Dungeons & Dragons. He was also very interested in Ted Bundy and the Blue Creek murderer. He was one of the few kids from my classes that I talked to, although I never talked to him out of class.

He moved to Tacoma with his sister and mother in my senior year and, right after we graduated, Walter jumped off the Narrows Bridge and killed himself.

At school, Walter Mitchell always stood with a few other D&D players near one of the boys' bathrooms on the main hall. Sometimes Walter's twin sister Susan stood there also, stared at by the other players, while Walter just smiled.

In Mr. Cavanaugh's biology class, I liked sitting behind Walter Mitchell, waiting for him to turn in his seat and begin telling me quietly and excitedly about Ted Bundy and the Blue Creek murders. Walter Mitchell was the strangest person I knew. With his slightly pale face and slightly messy hair, Walter sat listing off statistics, facts and trivia on Bundy and Blue Creek. Laughing lightly and shaking his head, throwing his hands up in horror or excitement.

Walter Mitchell led a volunteer group of high school and junior high kids that helped the police look for clues after murders. They would line up four feet apart, moving from one end of a crime scene to another, walking slowly, staring down, searching. They took weekend trips to Blue Creek, a place halfway between Tacoma and Seattle where the Blue Creek murderer had dropped prostitutes and other young women over the few decades before he was caught and where people like Walter Mitchell could still find bones and the shreds of clothing of unidentified victims. And sometimes Walter and his group went down to the gulch, when dead people turned up there.

But more than the random murders, Walter really liked talking about Ted Bundy and the Blue Creek murderer, because they'd both grown up in Tacoma. Bundy's family lived in my neighborhood. Walter Mitchell thought Bundy was a sicko. "There is no doubt about that," Walter would say in biology. But to Walter Mitchell, Ted Bundy was a kind of star. "There aren't many stars from Tacoma," he would say. "Bing Crosby, Frank Herbert. Go ahead. Name another."

"Bundy went to this high school," I'd always tell Walter, every time bringing a smile to Walter's face. "Everyone says Bundy seemed like a normal guy."

"I know," Walter would say, shaking his head. "I know."

"My dad knew the Blue Creek murderer," I'd tell Walter and he'd sit in his seat, shaking his head again, smiling even more.

"During their senior year," Walter would say

to me, because I'd told him this many times, but each time he liked to talk about it as if it were news to both of us. "In this class. Mr. Cavanaugh's class. Don't you think there's a kind of magic in that?"

Even back when my dad was in his class, Cavanaugh had long gray hair and always wore a bright orange hunting vest. Walter Mitchell and I could usually smell beer on Cavanaugh at seven-thirty in the morning, days when he'd sometimes take the embryo of a pig from a jar of formaldehyde and wave it around the room, the wrinkled, pink body dripping on the girls Cavanaugh always had seated in the front row, girls like Walter's sister Susan, the pig stinking up the room as it dripped formaldehyde on her and everyone in the front row, all of them leaning back in their seats until Cavanaugh finally dropped the pig back in its jar. On the days he'd been drinking, Cavanaugh would talk about how girls used to wear miniskirts and no underpants and how from the front of the class he could see it all. He talked about the reproduction of cells and about how boys needed to wear jock straps and girls needed to wear bras and that's just a fact, he would say, because the sexes are different.

And Walter would sometimes smile and shake his head and whisper to me, "The Blue Creek murderer heard this. In his formative years. Think of it."

And when Cavanaugh told the miniskirt story, I'd think about how my mother was in that class, too. Some empty face sitting near the Blue Creek murderer and my dad. Some person I can barely imagine. Some girl soon to be pregnant with me.

It was the day after Walter Mitchell killed himself that I found out some girl from The huts had
gotten pregnant and she'd have to have an abortion. She called me every few hours, crying and
saying she was pregnant. Saying she would have to
have an abortion.

All I can remember saying to her was a very
quiet, Well, okay, I think it's going to work out.

I'd heard of people who'd had abortions. Will
Wilson had paid for one that fall. It had always
seemed like a dirty thing. Something you shouldn't
talk about. But with this girl I was mostly scared.
Scared she'd have it. I went next door to Teddy's,
knocked on his window and woke him up to see if
he wanted to go for a drive.

It was a few days before I was supposed to
leave for Alaska with Kyle.

Teddy and I had first started our drives when
we were thirteen and neither of us had a license,
Teddy using his cousin's small pickup as just me
and him went driving around Tacoma. We would
drive aimlessly, the two of us sitting, staring out
the windows. Teddy always wanting to listen to the
sweet ballads on his favorite Seattle radio station.
Music that should have embarrassed Teddy and
me, but that Teddy listened to for hours out of the
one dashboard speaker that worked in his cousin's
old truck.

But as we'd turned fourteen and begun spending even more time with Will Wilson, I became less
interested in the drives, wanting instead to go by

Will Wilson's house, wanting to call and meet him, to see what he had going on, what he was thinking, what he could make happen. And Teddy always agreed.

We rode with the windows open now, eighteen and the June night air swirling cool and wet around us in the car. It was raining hard, the windows blurry and the road barely brightened by the car headlights. Water bursting over the hood of the car, hitting the windshield like a loud spray of pellets. Old Town to Parkland, turning back to cross the Tide Flats, Teddy driving on toward the Browns Point lighthouse. The two of us not talking, Teddy quietly humming along with the songs on the radio. Teddy was waiting for me to speak. Not looking when I started to cry. Not saying a word. Teddy would have driven all night with me.

And some time after Browns Point, I did tell him what happened. He nodded and said, *Okay, Brian.*

We hit a puddle in the road, the front tires cutting into it with a sound like tearing canvas, the car shaking, veering slightly, then catching the pavement again.

"I used to be pretty religious when I was a kid," Teddy said to me. "Sometimes I think about praying now. But when I think about it, I end up thinking about all I've done. That we've done, Brian. And I can't pray about one thing. It's just all of it. And it's just too much."

I was wiping at my face with my hand.

"Do you think about having kids someday?"

he asked.

"Christ, Teddy," I said, turning to him. "I don't want to think about that."

"Yeah. I know," he said, pushing his curly hair off his forehead. "But. Well, I think you should. And I should and Will Wilson and Coe should. I just mean that it's a little kid you could have had. A little boy or girl."

"Teddy, don't do that," I said.

"It's just the truth, Brian."

I stared out the windshield, seeing the wipers sweeping through the water.

"We're fucking up really bad," Teddy said.

And in a minute, I nodded. Not able to say yes. Not wanting to admit that what Teddy said was true, that somewhere inside I thought like him – thought not about God or praying, but thought that if I admitted even one act was wrong, admitted it even to myself, then everything would come apart, then all the things I'd done would hit me and push me down and never let me up.

All I thought I could do was fight to put everything behind me. To not even think about the last thing this girl had said to me. "If it was anyone else," she said, voice flat and quiet over the phone, "I'd probably keep it."

Teddy's car turned up a hill, away from the abandoned copper smelter, winding up the slope toward Point Defiance, passing half a block from the tall, brown smokestack, the car then cutting across the edge of the North End, past the bright gas stations and convenience stores. Heading us through near empty Sunday streets to wealthy Fircrest where you never speed because the cop cars are waiting. Passing through University Place where there's an all-night Denny's restaurant that we sometimes went to, crossing under an elevated section of Highway 16 and down into the sweet garlic air from the vats of pickle brine in the Nalley Valley. And even at the speed limit, the car seemed to race across the small blue bridges spanning the Tide Flats canals, the water below us reeking with a smell like broken sewer pipes, and in the canals were the ships loading and unloading logs and trucks, locomotives and oil, the radio reception getting bad as we wound along the curving roads leading to Browns Point. And at the lighthouse the two of us got out of the car to look at Tacoma. Standing in the cool wind from the bay, looking across water covered with a black sky of stars. We saw the Old Town hillside of yellow-lit streets and step-like blocks of two and three-story staggered houses, saw the spotted patterns of the houses' bright, square windows. And that night at Browns Point felt like the first time in years that I saw the city from a distance. That I wasn't packed in between houses, not shut in under streetlights, not standing below the dark Proctor Bridge. Not running fast along the bottom of the wet and black gulch.

And as we looked back at Old Town, Teddy and I didn't talk about all the houses we'd gone into there. We just stood together, staring out.

"Do you think you'll do anything with school?" Teddy asked. He shrugged. "Like going to college."

"No," I said. "What the fuck would I do in college? And then what? So I've gone to college. Fuck that."

And I also remember that night and that drive because at Browns Point Teddy then quietly told me he was thinking about going to college. Going to community college first, maybe in Seattle. Then trying to get into Washington State University, in eastern Washington, three hundred miles away.

And as he told me this I nodded and was quiet.

We were crossing the Tide Flats again to the waterfront at low tide, the wet and salty, heavy bay smell pouring through the windows. We were quiet again. But now it was a kind of answer. Teddy, who'd never thought school was important, needed my encouragement to go to college. Teddy, who seemed as bound to Tacoma and Will Wilson as deeply as me, needed my support to leave. Even to Seattle. Especially to eastern Washington. Teddy was trying to make a break. But that night I gave him nothing.

And I do still wish that I was quiet because I'd been afraid of losing my childhood friend. But really I was quiet because I wanted my life in Tacoma to remain intact, wanted all three of them, Will Wilson, Coe and Teddy, there for me.

The two of us shot along the dark bay bordered by the remnants of old mills, a mess of collapsed buildings that stood on black creosote pilings. Beyond the pilings on the far side of the bay was the Browns Point lighthouse, fifteen minutes away.

And then Teddy talked quietly about how he was going to ask out a girl named Pam that summer. She was a girl from one of his classes who he talked to sometimes. After seeing her, Teddy would come up to me in the hall and smile real bright and say things like, "She's really nice, Brian." Teddy had never been on a date. And when he mentioned her that night in the car, I realized that this girl Pam was going to school in eastern Washington, at Washington State. Like Teddy now wanted to do.

I stared out my window at the railroad tracks, turned and saw the gulch hillside above us.

A week before, Will Wilson had had sex with this girl. Pam. She'd been staggering drunk at a big graduation party. Teddy was at dinner with his parents. Will Wilson had started joking with Pam, trying to coax her out of a bedroom where she lay out on the floor. Saying to her, "Teddy's waiting. Teddy wants to see you."

And the thing is, she got up, she smiled. She followed Will Wilson outside.

Teddy hadn't told Will Wilson he liked this girl. I had.

The two of us were silent now, for twenty, thirty minutes, Teddy and I finally driving up Mc-Carver Hill toward our small houses above Old Town, driving past the step-like rows of nice homes, the reflection of the yellow streetlights glowing on the hood, the reflection of a house sometimes even shining on our windshield. McCarver Hill, which we'd driven up in an old Datsun pickup truck when we were thirteen years old, back then talking happily as we pointed out the open windows of the car, back then talking about being little kids, saying do you remember that bush on that corner where we found that whole box of Popsicle sticks? Do you remember the day we skipped school and walked through that alley and then that alley to cross just an edge of the gulch, going to the waterfront with the sand and the rock crabs? Thirteen and talking about childhood, saying do you remember the lady who lived in that house, who gave everyone the cocoa on snowy days? Do you remember that kid in the window of that house, how he'd smoke pot and stare, just stare out his window for hours, how he was there at the start of that walk and when we got back? Do you remember racing sticks down this hill in the rain, this very spot on this very block, me and you chasing boats, right here, right there, eight years old and passing through this car, me and you in a race at one hundred and twenty-five miles an hour?

I rolled down the car window and stuck my head into the rain, the spray from the road splashing against my chin, drops soaking my hair, stinging my face. In a minute, I brought my head inside. Wiped my face on my sweatshirt, pushed my wet hair out of my eyes.

I had my head and face back in the car, was wiping the rainwater on my sleeves.

"Will Wilson doesn't like that you're going to Alaska," Teddy said. "He thinks you should be staying here with us."

Will Wilson, Teddy and Coe were working at the port that summer. Will Wilson's step-dad had gotten us new jobs there, good jobs that paid a lot of money.

I hadn't told Will Wilson I wasn't staying with them. I sat in Teddy's car and wondered how he knew I was going to Alaska.

The car stopped in front of my house. The engine still running. Teddy said quietly, "Will Wilson was blowing up some old toaster this morning."

Teddy didn't talk for another minute. I held onto the door handle, thinking Teddy must have something more to say. Will Wilson was always blowing things up.

"And an old gas can," Teddy said quietly, "and this little TV. Two M-80s each. He called me at six this morning. Said he was blowing stuff up. Told me to come over."

Teddy was leaning against his door, turned as if looking toward me but staring out the windshield toward my house. The light from the radio glowed above my knee. Quiet music played from the dashboard.

"It's like I can't say no," Teddy said. "Going over there at six. I'd rather be in bed. But I can't say no."

I didn't say anything, just looked out the window. I could feel Teddy staring. Wanting me to agree.

"He was talking about break-ins and all," Teddy said, his voice loud now and awkward. "I don't know. It's like he's maybe pushing for something more."

I stared ahead, the intersection glowing pale yellow from a streetlight, the roads leading into it all lost in shadows. In a moment, I asked, "Like what?"

"I don't know. He was just talking. All quiet like he gets. Taping M-80s to this toaster. He unscrewed the back of this TV. You should have seen that TV go."

"What was he saying, though?"

"Like, I don't know," Teddy said, turning the radio up slightly. "I love this song."

"Come on, Teddy," I said.

"Just more, you know? When we're in the house. Things he's thinking about for when you get back. I don't know. He blew up an old, wooden mail box. It caught fire."

I sat in the car, staring at the shadows beyond the intersection. I knew Will Wilson was making decisions. Will Wilson was thinking, wishing.

I closed my eyes.

Will Wilson knew I was going to Alaska.

And I knew I should never come back.

And I knew, already, what was happening.

And I knew what Will Wilson wanted, even before Teddy said it.

Teddy's face looked a little pained, talking now like he was answering a question. "More," he said, shrugging. "Just doing more. I'm not sure about it. Like, I don't know. He was saying stuff. While, like, he was blowing these things up. Six a.m."

I lowered my head. Saw my feet. "Come on, Teddy."

"Just saying," Teddy went on, but getting quiet now and his voice evening out. "When we're in the house. Doing more. I'm not sure about it. Like, I don't know, Brian. Like waking people up."

•

Kyle was friends with Walter Mitchell's sister, Susan. They were a lot alike, something quiet and different and good about them. It stood out then, in Tacoma, and it does now too. I think probably they'd have been together if they'd had time that spring and summer, when we all were graduating and Kyle had lined me and him up with the jobs at the fish plant in Alaska.

Susan seemed older, seemed like she was in her twenties, and seeing her you'd think that, think she was probably twenty-three not eighteen, and that she had nothing for you, no time or interest. But really she was just quiet and not someone who brought a lot of attention to herself. This was hard for her, I think now, because she was so pretty that she always had a lot of attention. Kyle liked that a lot about her, that she didn't look for the attention she got. Probably because Kyle got that attention too, for the same reasons, that he seemed older and was good looking and seemed like someone you couldn't get to know.

They'd done acid together a few times, Kyle had told me. That was a thing, to do acid together,

to find someone who could get acid you could trust
or mescaline if you wanted, and Kyle had lived in
Tacoma his whole life, and so he could do both. Better, though, was meeting someone who liked it the
way you did, who liked to take a day and a night
and just go through the whole of it, in a park or near
the waterfront, watching the afternoon rain come
in over the bay and watching the sunset through
breaks in the clouds in the sky, finding someone to
do that with, that was a thing.

That's what Kyle told me about Susan, later.

And I'd done that with Kyle, at the Cispus
River.

Now Kyle and Susan had done acid a few
times, not too much, but enough, four times or five,
and so they had that, together.

The night I first talked to her she had come
down to the old docks that the fishermen still used.
Failing wooden marinas attached by three ramps
to the oily shore near the oil refinery. It smelled of
gasoline and burning chemicals and the boats that
were here were mostly not used anymore. There
was another marina, newer and smaller, that the
few fisherman still working out of Tacoma used.
But most of the fisherman had moved to the big
marina in Seattle and more still didn't even bother
fishing Puget Sound anymore. They fished Alaska,
year round, and that was enough.

Susan was looking for Kyle.

I'd been awake for a few days, with Will Wilson and Coe and Teddy, but had found my way
here, a few days before Kyle and me were supposed

to leave for Alaska.

I was thinking I had to tell him I wasn't going. There was no way I could go.

I knew of Susan from a few classes, from school, and knew of her because of Walter, her brother. But I'd never talked to her.

She told me later she thought I was someone else.

Kyle had been working to fix up his dad's old boat, the gill netter his dad had used for twenty years and that he'd left to Kyle when he died and that Kyle had only that year taken ownership of from his mother. A 24-foot boat, all wood, with a wheelhouse and cabin in the bow and a back deck and stern that were open now, without nets or any gear. Kyle had spent the last two weeks sanding and painting and cleaning.

Susan and I had both come down to find Kyle that night, Susan and me both parking in the weak yellow light of the parking lot, getting out of our cars and nodding some at each other, and saying we were looking for Kyle.

It was a night without temperature. Late spring, not warm yet but not cold.

We had to climb a metal fence and swing down to the ramp strung across the quiet, thick water of the waterway. I followed her down the ramp toward the old warehouses that were mostly unused now, following her as we passed through the narrow alleys between buildings and through open doors under tall wooden roofs, Susan in front of me, moving up and down stairs, turning sometimes to look at the ceiling, spinning farther and I had a glimpse of her face giving a slow flash of a smile, then still turning and she was gone, I could tell, her face and eyes showed it, she was for that moment somewhere else. I'd been drinking for days and later she told me she'd done acid too much, three or four times that week too.

Her brother, Walter, had just killed himself.

And we walked and I glanced into what I thought was another vacant warehouse and Susan and I both saw Kyle in the white light of a single bulb. Still in his clothes, on a mattress on the floor. Asleep after two weeks working on his father's old boat.

Pale light. A pile of tools. Kyle's duffel bag of work clothes for Alaska.

I could remember Susan and me turning from Kyle on the floor, me following Susan down a hall, outside to the docks. The moths circling the bulb on top of a cracked wooden pier. Seagulls for a moment screaming as they launched themselves from a nearby oil tank, then silent as they flew away. There was Kyle's dad's boat, wooden and damp and slick to the touch. And I can remember Susan in a flannel shirt open at her chest, stepping up onto the boat, can remember a second when she closed her bright eyes, pushed the dark hair from her face, and I can remember those sheets on the small bed built into the cabin, Kyle's sheets from when he was a kid, rodeo sheets with cowboys on horses and cowgirls on ponies.

It was months later that I slept with her. But

it started that night, that moment, when we were alone on Kyle's boat.

"What did you talk about with my brother?" she asked.

"Ted Bundy," I said. "The Blue Creek murderer."

"Walter wasn't well," she said.

"He seemed okay," I said. "I liked him," I said.

She nodded and smiled a little. "I'm glad," she said. "But Walter wasn't well."

I nodded. I was trying to say something to her, about him being dead, but I didn't know what would make sense.

"You're going to Alaska with him," she said. "With Kyle."

I nodded. "I guess," I said. "Yes," I said.

"You'll get away," she said. "It'll all be different."

"Yes," I said. "I think Kyle wants to make it different."

She stood and touched her face with her hands, then took her hands away. "Kyle told me he's trying to save you," she said, and she smiled a little and looked at me again. "But he didn't tell me what he's saving you from."

I nodded. Nodded. Closed my eyes. Nodded. "Some people," I said. "Some things."

"A lot of things then," I heard her say.

I sat down, then laid down on the bed where she'd been sitting, warm there, eyes closed, I thought I could sleep, I thought it'd be good to sleep. And I knew I would leave with him, in the morning. I didn't know how I couldn't.

"I'm afraid of him," I said.

"Of Kyle?" I heard her say.

"No," I said. "The other one."

"What other one?" I think I heard her say.

"A lot of things," I said, I think, but maybe I was already asleep.

4 DRIVING AWAY

It seems like we've been doing acid all day. On the drive, in a field, a day spent on acid in the sunlight of a cloudless sky. Driving and not talking, and sitting and not talking, and there, somewhere near Dale Creek, Wyoming, it seems like this will be okay.

Now, though, hours later, Kyle has disappeared. Gone in the crowd at some parking lot carnival I saw from the highway.

I'm twelve hundred miles from Tacoma. I've known all day that I'm going back. To meet her.

Before he disappeared, Kyle turned to me, where we stood in the shadow of a screaming haunted house in the center of this carnival.

"I didn't take any acid," he said.

I turn to him. I nod.

"I didn't take anything at all," he said to me.

I nod.

"Why are you here?" he said to me.

I nod.

"And why," he said, "why do you have me here too?"

I nod.

"When we were kids we wanted to take road trips," he said to me. "To go far away," he said. "But we only did that once."

I nod.

"And so," he says.

I turn away from him. Nod again. Close my eyes. Cover my eyes. Sit down. Lean forward. Press harder on my eyes. "And so," I say. "Why are you here?"

When we'd first driven in, though, it'd been different. We'd seen the carnival glow from the highway nearby and turned to each other, saying we needed to go, we had to see. Turning from the highway to the off ramp and to the main road here outside Cheyenne. Seeing wooden buildings, flat roofs, cinder block braces under a dismantled car. People walking, people watching. Watching us, it seemed, as we drove past them toward the same carnival each one of them was going to see.

"Turn," Kyle was saying, watching it all around us.

"Turn," I said.

The car moved so slowly, the speed of the highway gone. The buildings were bright with windows and signs, the black asphalt streets glowing with low streetlights. People passing under them. People laughing and walking and drinking and all of them making their way toward the glow of the carnival past the cars on the street, the cars lined up ahead of us, crawling toward the lights and the rides we could see.

"It's like a circus," Kyle was saying, the car turning as he looked at me, two women's faces passing so close to my window. "A circus, Brian."

There was music outside, drifting toward us

from the rides, music turning, building, ready to fall.

Kyle was talking slowly, dragging out sounds. "Ringling Brothers and Barnum and Bailey," he was saying.

I leaned forward, looking up out the windshield. Trying to see the night sky, but not seeing past the low buildings. Not even seeing past the lights.

"Circus Romani," Kyle was saying. "The Big Apple Circus." He turned to me. Smiling like a child. "Come on, Brian. Help me remember. It's the name of a circus."

The music had stopped and the colors of it still all spun through the bumps of the car over the potholes in the road, through the growing noise of the people outside of our windows.

I could see four people dancing in a circle in an alley. Could see a tall man balanced on the edge of a curb.

"Unusually agile people walking across brightly painted barrels," Kyle was saying. "Manic depressives in big clothes and heavy make up. The Big Apple Circus, Brian. The Clyde Beatty, Cole Brothers Circus."

The road was over. The ride was done.

"I see the open door of a small car," I heard Kyle say, smiling at me, touching my arm. "A clown in wide shoes stepping loudly into the tent. Another stepping with force, bouncing with a smile. Crossing quickly to the screaming stands of the children."

The ride, I'd now realized, where we'd been safe. Where, in a way, nothing could happen.

"I have always hated the circus," I finally said to him. Turning to Kyle and smiling. "You know I hate the circus."

"Clowns in cars," Kyle was saying. "Clowns on ponies."

"I always hated when they'd leave the rings," I was saying. "When they'd come into the stands."

"The rest of the audience always seemed so excited," Kyle was saying, smiling.

"I always felt like they were coming for me," I was saying.

Kyle's hand reached toward me, the car slowing now. "The Shriners," he was saying, holding my arm. Squeezing me, remembering. "Circus Circus," he was saying. "The B&I. It's the one out West, Brian," he was saying. "When we were kids," he was saying, smiling wider then, and nodding and all the while Kyle was looking at me, holding my arm, nodding yes, yes.

"I know," I was saying. "I know. It's the one from Alaska. The one I couldn't visit. The one called Circus Vargas."

I turn away from Kyle. The car is right next to the rides now, coin-operated rides for little kids. I look back and Kyle is not the car. Outside his window, I see a small boy riding a coin-operated horse, the Lone Ranger theme playing, the scratchy music mixed with the gallop of a hundred hooves. And the car is stopped, me watching the boy out the window and his mother glances at me and at first she is smiling but in a moment she turns her eyes away, not smiling, and I see her cross her arms across her chest, as if holding herself for a moment.

And I know I still smell of violence. Remember right then what it is to care about no one but myself. Remember how I enjoyed how we looked and how we smelled and how we could cause fear.

Kyle is gone. But still I am staring at that boy on his horse, hanging onto its neck with both his small arms, the blue and white animal leaping forward in place, the boy floating up and down with the motion, his face carrying that nearly numb smile of quiet realization, the boy maybe right then waking up to the world, becoming conscious of his life, creating memories he'd one day view.

And the mother is standing in front of him, smiling at him and waving her hand. Saying, "Bye, bye," she says. Saying, "Bye, bye. Bye, bye."

4   RETURNING

She is nearing a city. There are more cars now, and many lights.

She's remembering this place. Remembering how from the stern of the boat she could see the refinery, half a mile from where they'd been tied to a tilting wooden pier, a cold night in the dim reflection of the city, the flat black water somehow pure, unbroken between here and the refinery, the flames of the pipes lifting up against the sky, orange and red and blue in flashes, reflecting off that smoothest surface of the bay, silent except for a car along the waterfront beyond the pier and a truck on the hill working hard up the slope to the city of neighborhoods beyond what she could see and farther still the echoing scream of a machine among the refineries or the pulp mills, somewhere in those miles of tanks of fuel and turning parts and falling smoke, black or gray, smoke so heavy it fell, thickness that glowed bright in the halo of lights placed high above the work that went on.

And she remembers how she started to look back, toward the bow of the boat and the black oily refuse of the piers along the bay and the hillside of darkened houses and the gulch of woods and brush.

But she would not turn back, because she

would not turn back toward him, the boy she'd been with, spread out, inside her. She would only take another bit of paper, this time she'd take two, on her tongue, where it would melt as she pressed it against the smoothest surface of her teeth, not watching, not seeing, not hearing him as he slept, but instead she was alone, watching the still, black water off the stern of this old boat.

That boy, naked, passed out in a bunk below, asleep after crying, not himself, she thought, not at all.

But, then again, he'd been through a lot.

And even though she'd swam, diving into the water, cold and swimming, kicking her legs as hard as she could, even still she could feel it, inside her, wet. Moving. Making its way deeper still.

And now, in her car, years later, she was nearing the city. Nearing Tacoma.

Her brother had killed himself and her mother had already done it to herself, a year earlier, after they'd moved, and the aunt they'd first gone there to live with, she'd barely been able to keep food in the house.

When she was eighteen and first moved to this place, this Tacoma, she heard stories about Will Wilson and the other three. How the four of them had been driving fast on the bright empty roads at the Tide Flats since they were kids. How the four of them got in fights and they hurt people who they didn't like. How they hurt these people bad. How there were girls, too, somehow there were always girls. And how in all this they were so quiet. Just so fucking quiet.

But when she moved to Tacoma, it was a while before she'd heard all their names. Will Wilson and Porter and Ted Selva and Coe. She never heard Michael. Never heard Teddy. Never heard Brian.

And, really, Susan didn't think much about Will Wilson or the others. She'd sat near Brian, met him twice, before she heard his last name.

He seemed okay. Her brother liked him. And Kyle liked him too.

That mattered most of all.

And, anyway, it's the other one she really loved. Kyle. Still, even now, she wishes it had been Kyle.

5 NOW
WITH KYLE
TACOMA
DRIVING AWAY
RETURNING

5 NOW

Around our neighborhood, people are very nice and they cook out or eat dinner on porches, and when they do they always offer me and her beer. We're water people, she'll say, and can say it in a way I wouldn't be able.

I'd make it sound dramatic, bad, and you'd find yourself wondering if it was really that big a deal.

She just says, No, thanks.

I had to leave Wyoming. One more step away. I knew someone who could get me a job here in Missouri. And from that job I started running the lumberyard.

She's a good person, not a perfect one, who I like to be with, who heard my stories and had stories of her own.

It's been really good for my daughter.

Not that I wouldn't have made it work on my own. Because I would have

5   WITH KYLE

After dinner in Kenai, Alaska, we went outside into the gray light and crossed the gravel parking lot to the highway to hitch a ride back to Sterling. It was Sunday and we'd had dinner in town and played pool for a few hours and pinball for as long as Kyle would let me.

It was a few minutes and this old rusting Ford pickup stopped and there was a man and woman in the front and these two kids in between them and a real big German Shepherd in the back.

We climbed over the side into the bed and sat leaning against the cab. The truck pulled out onto the road and cool air was blowing down my shirt and I reached and snapped it up all the way to the collar.

I looked at the dog then and he was staring at me. I was wondering if maybe I was in his territory and he didn't like that and then he lunged forward and licked me real fast across my mouth and eyes and forehead. Kyle was laughing. The truck was bouncing on the road and I was wiping my face with the sleeve of my denim jacket and the dog was now just hanging its head and paws over the side of the truck.

The wind behind the cab was swirling and it blew hair across my eyes. I pushed it back with my hand, but already the wind blew the hair over my eyes again and so I sat, hand on my face, staring out at the gray and yellow and blue sky and the mountains and the tall clouds that seemed to sit just above the horizon.

It wouldn't get totally dark in this part of Alaska during early July and Kyle said it wouldn't start getting dark again till August. The sunsets went on for hours and the colors of the sky kept slowly changing, through evening and night and it was real hard to fall asleep, but that was okay.

No one told me it'd be light all the time in Alaska. I guess they used to tell us in school that the sun didn't go down up here in the summer, but I didn't really expect it to be like that.

As we rode I took my wallet from my back pocket and opened it up. I counted fifty-three dollars and put the wallet back. Fifty-three dollars was only enough money for about a week's worth of food and a few beers a night. We hadn't made much money yet. Four weeks in and only a few hundred dollars. The other guys around the plant were worried and I was worried but Kyle kept saying it'll be fine.

And then this dog decided to switch sides and he walked across me like I wasn't even there, stepping on my stomach and my legs. Kyle didn't laugh this time. He was nodding toward the side of the road, and I saw a moose standing. The dog was barking at it now. Calling to it maybe. I wasn't sure, but he barked for a few minutes, quietly though, with the wind blowing.

We were climbing a hill and I could hear the engine working harder. I reached over and scratched the dog's neck. He'd settled down now, head facing back toward the sunset. Kyle was slowly peeling fish scales from his arm, lifting the thin silver circles into the wind and letting them fly. The dog didn't seem to notice me and I kept scratching him. I liked it that way, just pushing my fingers through his fur and feeling his warm skin and not having him licking me or anything. I just wanted to keep pushing my hand through his fur, pushing and rubbing along his neck.

We rode that way, about half an hour, and then we were back to our camp site above the processing plant.

•

I woke up in the morning with the sun shining in on my face through a rip in my tent. I pulled on some jeans and unzipped the tent and crawled outside. The sun was shining through the trees but it was still cold outside. I looked at my watch. Seven-thirty.

I opened my ice chest and took out the carton of milk and then spread some peanut butter on a couple pieces of white bread. I walked through the trees and down the little incline and then up onto the dirt ridge that looked down on Red Salmon Processing and the Kenai River.

There were already people down on the river with their poles fishing. Some of them were in hip boots and were maybe five or ten feet out into the river, just dark spots in the whitish yellow reflection of the sun. Kyle was down there. I remembered him waking up a few hours earlier.

I finished the bread and drank down some milk, looking over toward the plant. There was the big, yellow wood building where they did the canning and the two green aluminum buildings, one where they froze and one where they processed.

I was hoping for fish, even saying the word quietly to myself, closing my eyes for a second.

There'd been maybe a thousand fish caught for our plant in the four openings the commercial fishermen had had. A thousand fish was nothing. A thousand fish was a wasted summer.

I went back to the tent. I put on a shirt and hat and my wool socks and boots and then walked down to the plant.

I hung around in the break room drinking coffee with about seven or eight other guys, all of them older than me. Kyle came in after about half an hour, smiling some and I knew he'd caught some fish on the river.

A couple guys were playing cards and some others were talking, but for the most part it was pretty quiet. A couple times the plant manager Jack walked by the door but he just sort of nodded and didn't say anything. The secretary brought mail in to some of the guys who were living in tents and having their mail delivered to the plant. Kyle had a letter to send, like he did about once a week, and he gave it to the secretary with some change so she could send it.

A few minutes later Jack came in and shook his head, raised his hands. He left. No fish again today.

We all stood and walked outside.

Kyle slept a lot through the rest of the day. I couldn't, though. I fished at the river and caught a salmon. It seemed like kind of a kid thing, catching fish with a pole on the river, but I was laughing when I got the fish and managed to pull it into a bucket and I leaned over it longer than I meant to, staring down, touching it's smooth silver side, hand gliding easy across skin like metal and the scales on my fingers were nearly clear and were so bright in the sun.

•

We spent the next couple days the same way, on the river and going to town some nights, and in the mornings going to Red Salmon and waiting around. But there weren't any fish.

I had just twenty dollars now and we had a loaf of bread and some milk and peanut butter. Kyle was napping more now. And finally one day I laid down on the ground outside the tent, middle of the day, not meaning to sleep, just having nothing else to do, and I woke up a few hours later, a dreamless timeless sleep.

Then another morning came and we went down to the plant and there was fish. I smelled it first, before I even got there. It was all around me as we got close, thick and bitter, a taste in my mouth.

At the plant there were white plastic totes stacked four high in the processing room and a truck in the yard was carrying another twenty. The totes were about five feet by five feet and three feet tall and there was blood on the outside of most and on some you could see the black shadows of the fish pressed against the insides. There were a lot of guys around too, some of them like me, just standing and looking at the totes, a few others on fork lifts moving the fish around.

Most of us went into the processing room and Jack was in there pulling new rubber gloves and aprons out of boxes and handing them out to people.

And then the machines started up. The gutting machine with the saw blades screaming as they started to spin and the guillotine snapping down and the plastic conveyor belt rattling and everywhere around me the sound of water pouring. There was water in tanks along the conveyor and in the gutting machine and running past the guillotine and leaking down from pipes above the racks.

People were yelling for the fish and I heard the fork coming in with the first tote. Guys were yelling louder now and I was clapping my hands together and nodding my head.

Kyle and I were racking fish, end of the processing line, where you put the fish on trays before they're sent to the freezer room.

The fish got dumped and the guy at the guillotine was sliding them into the slot and popping heads off with this thudding sound and there was the even higher whine of the gutting machine as the fish went through and now even more water, pouring out of the tanks and running under my feet toward the drain and dripping down onto everyone's heads.

And we processed fish all day. I racked slowly at first, Kyle laying the cut fish in the steel and plastic freezer racks faster than me. But I watched him hard and by midday I was going as fast as him. Sometimes I looked around and saw the guys cutting gills, their hands and arms and chests red with blood, and the girls doing roe, sitting under the gutting machine and sorting out the eggs while the water and guts poured over their hoods and down the backs of their rain gear. And sometimes I stared down at the guts all over the floor, an inch thick, yellow and brown, red and black.

And we stopped for lunch and again for dinner around six but we keep processing fish. At midnight Jack came in and hit the power and the machines stopped and people were turning off the water. My ears were ringing and my eyes were blurry and I couldn't really tell if my chest and arms were shaking or not. I took off my gloves and my hands were white and swollen from so much cold water and even with the apron the front of my shirt and jeans was wet to the skin.

We went up to our tent, my ears ringing and my head feeling real heavy. I ate two pieces of bread and pulled peanut butter from the jar with my hand and drank the rest of the milk to wash it all down.

My boots came off real easy and I sort of peeled off my wet socks and then I crawled into the tent. I tried to pull off my jeans but they were so wet it was too hard so I just rolled up with my sleeping bag on top of me. Kyle was sitting outside the tent, looking up at the night sky, but I had to close my eyes. And for a minute my ears rang and I smelled the fish on my clothes and skin and heard the water running and the guillotine thudding down and I could see thousands of them, silver and black, wet and bloody, all piled in front of me, so many that it's all I could see.

•

We worked sixteen hour shifts for the next three days, then a week, then the next two months. And for those next two months I went to sleep with my ears ringing, wet and exhausted and happy. There was money and there was so much work and so many fish. We hardly got a day's break, and that was okay, we didn't talk about it. No one did. We worked and sometimes we'd go to town for dinner and pool and once even there was a small parking lot carnival in the center of town, with rides we didn't go on, but we played some of the games and ate some of the food and walked around for an hour in the fading day's sunlight with all those kids screaming happily around us.

A carnival and a circus, with a small tent and animals and clowns inside, but we didn't go inside. I laughed but told Kyle I couldn't. Not a circus, even a little one, some forgotten low budget show called Circus Vargas.

I just couldn't go in that tent.

Kyle laughed at me, but it was okay.

In August I sat on the ridge near our tent looking down at the river and the plant. It was late, I knew, but I didn't know what time it was. The sky was turning gold off near the mountains and a wind was blowing steady against the current of the river, turning the water white in thin, curved lines.

After a while, Kyle sat down next to me. He'd cooked fish on the campfire and we ate a few pieces each, from our hands, too tired for plates, and it tasted better that way, from your hands, sitting quiet in the wind. Kyle's uncle had died, the old man from the boat blessing. It's sad, Kyle told me, but it's okay. It was going to happen.

And he told me he'd gotten his permit to fish in the San Juans that fall, in the gill netter that was his dad's, and he wants me to be his crew, and after that we can get on one of his cousin's boats, in Alaska again.

I say yes, of course. Of course I did. I say yes, thanks. Yes. Because it's all I've ever wanted.

5   TACOMA

We were back about a day when Will Wilson found me.

Early September and Will Wilson came to my house on a Wednesday night. Showing up around ten-thirty.

Will Wilson was wearing jeans. And a bright, white t-shirt.

He'd called me earlier and told me there was a party to go to. Some kid's house. I'd told him I wouldn't be home.

Will Wilson wandered through my room now, half full boxes all around the floor. I was packing to move out. Leaving for the San Juans the next day.

"Where's your sweatshirt, Porter?" Will Wilson asked, looking in my closet. "I hope you didn't pack the black one."

And I saw his dark shoes then. His hooded black sweatshirt hanging on my doorknob. His black gloves hanging from his back pockets. A bottle of bourbon on the floor near the door.

He turned to me and smiled. Hair to his shoulders. Face so hard. Dark eyes shining. Will Wilson said to me, "And bring your gloves."

Coe smiled. Teddy stared. And I drank more. Drank quietly, drank again, sitting and leaning toward the fire in front of us, feeling the heat and smoke in my eyes. Drank more and didn't show it to them, sitting low in my chair behind the flames at the fire on the high dark ledge under the Proctor Bridge.

"I want to wake someone up," Will Wilson said. "In the house. See what happens."

And I drank. Watching Will Wilson in the dim light, turning now to look over the high ledge above the gulch, the concrete arches under the bridge, reaching even higher, out into the darkness. Thinking about some house we would go into in Old Town, some house on the hill above the bay. Thinking about the four of us crossing the doorway, spreading out through the room, Teddy behind, Coe smiling wide, Will Wilson ahead of me, leaning forward slightly, staring ahead. The four of us stopping, waiting in the dining room or kitchen, the living room maybe. Listening for sound. For anyone moving. Quickly finding the foot of the stairs. Here in a house that Will Wilson would have picked, a house with people he had watched on his own. Walking by on the street, passing down their alley. Sitting in a car at the corner of their block. Watching. And inside the house we all would climb the stairs, Will Wilson first, the rest behind, each of us silently multiplied by the presence of the others. Wearing the masks from the garage fires. The leather gloves from so many other break-ins. The four of us moving down the dim, gray hallway, Will Wilson listening at bedroom doors. Listening for the sound he wanted. The sound, I was sure, of some teenage girl.

Will Wilson would know that the parents were away. He would know when they were coming back. Will Wilson would know. Will Wilson would find out.

Will Wilson pointing his leather fingers, Coe and Teddy sent to watch the doors.

Will Wilson and I opening the door to the girl's room.

Regret not possible. Decisions made. Waking her up in the night.

Tacoma was our city. And we were at the center. Everyone else was a part of our life. Everyone else was there for us.

Nothing was too much anymore. Nothing at all.

In a girl's room taking turns.

We would not be stopped. We would not get caught.

Near the fire I was drinking more of the bourbon, drinking again because I knew I would do it. I knew I would follow him into that house. Picking the lock if he asked.

Holding her mouth if I had to.

Next to the fire, I could see it all happening. Next to the fire, it was already done.

Kyle was on the ledge now. It was dark under the bridge but I could see it was him. I put the bottle down. I thought I should stand.

Will Wilson was only sitting, watching Kyle step forward.

I wasn't sure they'd ever met.

Will Wilson seemed to know why Kyle was

there.

They fought, but not really. Will Wilson stood up from the old lawn chair he'd been sitting in, moving toward Kyle, slowly, but I knew even then, so drunk in the dim light of that gap under the bridge across the gulch, the high ledge we'd been drinking on for so many years, that we'd played on when we were kids and that we'd met at so many times at the start of so many nights, I knew Will Wilson would not move slow for long, and already he'd slid right, right again, punching, punching.

The thing is, though, that Kyle only leaned back, took it, and after a few seconds grabbed Will Wilson, hard, by the arms and chest, and slammed him to the ground.

"You leave with me," Kyle said, looking at me, knees on Will Wilson's back, hands holding Will Wilson's arms down in the dirt.

Will Wilson said nothing. He couldn't move Kyle off him. The only fight he ever lost. And Kyle hadn't even hit him yet. The hitting started soon, though. But now Kyle was still talking to me. "You leave with me," he said again.

I stared.

Kyle hit Will Wilson in the side of the head, in the face, in the neck. He lifted his arms to Will Wilson's back and it was like he was going to break them, but didn't.

"You leave with me," he said again.

Will Wilson still said nothing. I could barely see his face. But it hurt. What Kyle was doing hurt.

Coe and Teddy were staring too. Because of

me, I think. Because I didn't get up. And when I didn't get up Coe especially didn't know what to do, was starting to rock in his seat, rock back and forth, and I could hear him moan.

I remember a lot of things, but mostly I remember wishing Kyle would kill him.

But he didn't.

And I didn't stand, or move to leave. I thought I should. I was just so drunk. It was so dark. And it was taking so much to understand what was happening.

Will Wilson finally slid out from under him, from Kyle, and he stood and he didn't kick Kyle or hit him or say anything, still. Will Wilson just pushed him off the ledge.

I got into the car like I had a few hours earlier. When Will Wilson first showed up at my house. Got into the car. All he did was ask.

The four of us were in his white Chevelle now, music playing thick and slow from the speakers. Teddy was in the back seat next to Coe. Teddy's voice came quiet. "Where are we going?" he asked.

"We have some time," Will Wilson said.

The rain was hitting the windshield, breaking the streetlight shine into red and blue. It was twelve o'clock. We were bouncing easily off the crests of the downtown hills when Teddy spoke again. Five minutes later. "I don't have the right clothes," he said.

The car lifted off a hill, the hum of the road disappearing, and for that second we flew.

"That's all right, Teddy," Will Wilson said, the

car hitting the road again, my head jerking slightly, the hill ending as we crossed Pacific Avenue. "I brought extras for you."

We hadn't looked over the ledge. But I was thinking that maybe it wasn't a high ledge. Not too high.

We were on the short bridge to the Tide Flats, the ripe smell of the pulp mill pouring through the windows. The rain shining wet on the road. Will Wilson was pushing the car harder, bringing us up to seventy-five then ninety-five miles an hour, the lights of the container ships and smokestacks turning to streaks around us as we hit one hundred and ten. The engine a solid roar above the music and wind. None of us speaking. Will Wilson not smiling. Only staring at the road. Both hands on the wheel, at one hundred and twenty-five, I leaned forward, working against the pressure of the speed, hand pulling on the dash as I looked up through the windshield, drinking a long burning taste from the bottle of bourbon, seeing the lights blurring to silver against Tacoma's night sky.

There was a power in that, too. The rushing speed. The silence between us all. The drink spreading fast, reaching down to my hands and legs, reaching through to my eyes. At fourteen, it had been enough power for me.

At eighteen, it didn't even come close.

I turned and saw Coe smiling just slightly. Saw Teddy only staring at Will Wilson in the mirror. Face empty. Not looking at me.

Will Wilson slowed before the turn to Browns

Point, taking us along the dark, winding road at the speed limit. He stopped the car in the parking lot at the lighthouse.

"We have some time," Will Wilson said again as we all got out of the car.

As a kid, I'd jumped off the ledge under the Proctor Bridge, like a slide you could ride down to a trail in the gulch.

The wind was blowing cool off the bay now, the low waves splashing lightly against the rocks on the beach.

Coe was drinking something from a clear glass bottle. Swallowing slowly. Blinking it away.

I opened a can of beer. I was watching Will Wilson pull a sweatshirt from the trunk. I could see a hat and gloves hanging from the sweatshirt's front pocket.

The night sky above the Tide Flats was lit brown by the stacks and warehouses, the sky on the far side of the dark bay lit pale yellow from the streets and houses in Old Town. Two jets circled the city, banking into their descent.

I wiped the thin layer of rain from my fore-head and eyes.

Teddy was standing next to me, staring at Will Wilson. "I won't do this," Teddy said quietly.

I couldn't say anything.

I'd slid down the ledge fifty times. As a kid it'd been fun.

I couldn't say anything to Teddy. I was going to do this. And not because Will Wilson demanded it.

That much more power.

Will Wilson stood in front of Teddy. Holding out the sweatshirt.

And it was a minute of Will Wilson smiling vaguely, staring hard at Teddy. Of Teddy looking out toward the bay and Old Town. Then Teddy turning to Will Wilson, saying, "No."

Will Wilson hit him once below the eye without the sweatshirt seeming to move.

Teddy was on the ground. Coe slowly stepped closer, drinking the clear liquid. Lips wet as he swallowed.

"I'm not going to," Teddy said, sitting up. "I'm not."

Will Wilson kicked him in the chest. Teddy fell over.

I stood watching. Slowly drinking from my beer.

"No, Teddy," Will Wilson said quietly. Almost nicely. "You're wrong, Teddy."

Teddy had sat up again, both hands pressed against his chest.

"Put it on, Teddy," Will Wilson said.

"I won't," Teddy said, sucking a breath between words. "I'm not."

Will Wilson swung hard, fist slashing down then away. The back of Teddy's head hit the pavement.

There'd been no sound from below the ledge, though. No sound down there at all.

Teddy hit the pavement again. I was thinking that Teddy had made his choice. Knowing Teddy would lose this one, too. Knowing he was on his own.

I finished my beer. Dropped the can on the ground. Reached for Coe's bottle.

Teddy was having trouble breathing now. His mouth hung partly open as he slowly looked around.

I swallowed white alcohol. Blinked the burn away.

I was thinking Teddy just needed to accept this. To accept that he wanted to do it. To accept that this would happen.

And I was thinking that there is only so much softness you can take. There is only so long you can side with a loser.

Teddy sat up. Shaking his head. "You did it. To Kyle," he said. "Fuck you, Will," he said.

His eyes rolled white as he was hit again, Will Wilson aiming from shoulder level, punching straight and down. Blowing a low, short breath as he connected.

Will Wilson carefully crouched down over Teddy. "No one will help, Teddy," he said. "Not even your neighbor."

I looked at Will Wilson. I drank from the bottle.

Will Wilson very slowly and almost delicately pulled Teddy up to sitting. "Come on, Teddy," he was saying quietly. "Come on."

Teddy's mouth was bleeding. He pawed at his teeth with his wrist. Will Wilson lifted one of Teddy's hands over his head. Pushed the sleeve of the sweatshirt down to the shoulder. Carefully slid Teddy's head into the hood.

Coe took the bottle from me.

"Come on, Teddy," Will Wilson was whispering, the wind blowing his long, straight hair off his shoulders. "Come on."

It took Will Wilson a minute to dress Teddy. Straightening out the sweatshirt. Holding each of Teddy's fingers as he fit them into the first of the black, leather gloves. "We're not going to hurt anyone," Will Wilson was saying.

Teddy stared back at him, carefully licking his wet, bloody lips.

"Who would we hurt?" Will Wilson was saying.

And I was drinking from the bottle of bourbon, picking it up from next to Will Wilson. Drinking and turning from him, seeing the bay and the rain and the lights of Old Town just fifteen minutes away.

"I would never hurt anyone," Will Wilson was saying, still crouched over, still straightening Teddy's clothes.

I saw Teddy's three fingers without nails, the skin at the tips grown white and callused since he'd lost them on the roof of a car, two years, three years, twenty years earlier. And now Will Wilson covered the hand with the other glove.

"It won't hurt at all," Will Wilson said. "Not at all, Teddy. Not at all."

We were crossing the Tide Flats at forty miles an hour, Will Wilson circling out past the junkyards and smaller saw mills. Only a few trucks drove on the wide, brightly lit streets. Our wipers moving slowly, clearing the thin layer of raindrops from the windshield.

The four of us were on our way to the house. Some house. The one Will Wilson had chosen for us.

I hadn't looked at Teddy. Hadn't turned around since we'd gotten back in the car at the lighthouse. I took a drink of the bourbon, the taste pale and warm, my eyes watering as I swallowed.

The stereo ground slowly on, voices trailing through music and noise.

I took a slow breath, the wet air brushing my numbed lips. And then I realized we were heading toward the highway. Away from Old Town.

We weren't going to do it. Not if we were leaving Old Town. Will Wilson was joking. Or testing. Because we were leaving Old Town. The four of us were just going to drive around, Will Wilson at the wheel, taking the long way to South Tacoma or the Narrows Bridge. We would drive and drink and maybe climb the bridge this night. Climb the bridge cables to the steel towers, toast bourbon and beer and look out over the city. Seeing the power towers where Clarence Stark had died and houses we'd broken into. Seeing the smelter smokestack where my grandfather had worked and seeing as far as the Tide Flats, where the four of us would all someday be. We would sit and stare and drive and Will Wilson and Coe and Teddy would smile and whatever Will Wilson had said, that would be just a thought. The violence of it gone. The force of it passed. The possibility eliminated. All but forgotten.

The car crossed under a freeway overpass, Will Wilson leaning forward, the car pushing hard toward the on-ramp.

And I rolled my window down farther, the cool, wet air blowing across my warm face. I leaned closer to the wind, the rain across my ears now and in my hair and I felt good that it wouldn't happen. Knew that this had been about a pain we'd never seen.

The car was moving on the highway now, moving maybe sixty miles an hour, safe and fast and the lights of downtown Tacoma shimmered white and gold and pale in my watering eyes.

And I turned from the window to look back at Teddy and smile but as I turned I stopped because I saw Will Wilson's lips wet with bourbon, one gloved hand holding the bottle by the neck, the other hand pushing into another black glove. Will Wilson driving with his knee. Staring at me. Smiling.

I didn't even look at Teddy. I was already turning back to the road. Will Wilson taking the exit to the highway extension, Shuster Parkway and the car accelerating to seventy. Seventy-five. Shooting through nighttime shadow of downtown Tacoma. Heading toward Old Town.

I was wrong. Will Wilson had made a decision. And we were five minutes away.

He turned the music up louder, the sound all

moaning and steady. No words, only rolling, only noise.

Will Wilson had made a decision. We would do this.

Shuster Parkway narrowed under an elevated road, the concrete supports passing near my window, the steel hum of the engine echoing hard off the cement overhead.

I stared at the gloves in my lap, the car lifting off a crest, my chest emptying as the tires connected with the road again and I rolled up my window as the car hit eighty, the air still tearing loud through Will Wilson's and Coe's open windows. The blue-white streetlights shining bright on the pavement, on the concrete walls to our side, the inside of the car lit gray and white and black. And past Will Wilson's sharp, staring face I could see the gulch above us, the trees and brush growing from a cliff-like hillside that dropped straight down from the huts.

Ninety-five. One hundred and five. Will Wilson's hair lifting from his head, blowing in streaks across his shoulders, reaching forward like cords toward the windshield. And he turned to me then, eyes white and black in the streetlight of the car.

"Before we're there," Will Wilson said to me, the sound so low under the music moaning and the wind ripping hard through the car. "Now, Porter, before we do it."

And Will Wilson was climbing out the window. His black sweatshirt gone, jeans disappeared.

And the smooth, white pavement stretched out ahead of us, the concrete of the low wall to the right and now the high wall to the left all passing us like it surrounded us. My foot on the gas. Car going faster. My hands not yet reaching for the wheel.

And I looked back then. To see Teddy. He was watching me. His face swollen, blood dried to his nose and around his right eye. His curly hair blown away from his face.

I could hear the tires thumping as they crossed the bumps of the center line. Could see the wall so close, the wall just a few feet away. Could feel the roof shaking, Will Wilson screaming and pounding, voice so far away. "Now, now, now."

Coe was smiling wide at the ceiling, turning to look at the untouched wheel, turning to the high concrete wall so close on our left. Coe yelling loud now. The sound from his chest and throat. The sound full and happy and all that he'd ever felt.

Teddy was shaking his head. Face blank. No. "Now, now, now."

I realized Kyle was dead. Of course he was.

I had my hand on the wheel as the car hit the wall. And we were bouncing fast away from concrete, my body thrown toward the steering wheel, hands and face smacking the pedals as the car hit the other wall, tires sliding loud, me looking up through the steering wheel, seeing Will Wilson's staring, still face pass the windshield before the car went quiet, my head and chest pushed so hard toward the pedals, my neck pinching and chest without air and my arm snapping fast, lifting to the wheel, the sound around me a nothing like my breath was nothing, glass breaking loud and steel grinding and my legs jammed under the seat and no breath, the noise everything, noise beyond the pain in my flapping arm and the pull against my legs and beyond the pressure of my face against the wheel and my neck wrenching hard and harder and the noise now gone again and Coe coming past me, legs hitting my chest and catching my side and pulling my arm hard with him to the window, breaking my arm again at the wrist, bloody white bone pointing through the skin, glass flying in a blue-white shimmer that came across my face like a fire, Coe gone and my body jerking hard away from everything, floating free beneath the seat and attached only at the neck, only where my jaw caught against the steering wheel, sound gone, the ceiling against the seat, metal against my side and the noise shaking through my chest and legs and the car screaming high with steel, screaming with the concrete grinding, screaming with glass still breaking, bits breaking more, shattering again, cutting across my arms again, the seat tearing loose and the car knocking and jerking and going silent, my head loose from the wheel, blood blowing bright across my mouth and eyes and my chest hitting hard against a seat, body snapped up to the ceiling or floor, the hit leaving me without air, without feeling how I could breathe, the car knocking hard again before going silent, lifted from anything, tumbling down Shuster, flipping once more.

Will Wilson, Coe and Teddy are dead.

After the fire department had pried away the roof, I very slowly walked away.

I remember lying in the ambulance breathing oxygen from a mask. Staring out the door as uniformed men and women asked me questions I couldn't answer. Because I couldn't talk. I could only try to breathe. But I could see the crushed, flattened car in the dirt. Could see, farther up Shuster, under the tall, pale streetlights, two groups of fire trucks and police cars.

The group a hundred feet away had be to be standing around Coe. The other group, farther still, had to be standing above Will Wilson.

I could remember the wreck so clearly. Lay there playing it back in my head.

I would read the police reports months later. Will Wilson and Coe each had their own pages filled with the details of their injuries. Both had died immediately when their necks broke against the concrete.

Teddy's report concluded that he'd died suddenly, too. Torn from the car at some point in the flipping. The fourth flip, the police thought. Possibly the fifth. Caught under the car. Near the axle. Scalp torn open. Skull cracked.

But in the quiet after the car had stopped moving, when I'd lain in the dark pulling slow, shallow breaths through my throat to my chest, I'd heard Teddy. Somewhere around me, maybe up or down, saying, "No. No." Stopping before I heard the sirens. Stopping before I could force words out of my mouth.

I think that all I could have said to him was, *It's okay, Teddy. You're okay, Teddy.* Just something to make him feel better.

Although I do hope he didn't feel a thing. I do hope he wasn't really conscious. I hope that, in its way, his body was barely functioning, was instead just numbly moving forward.

And Kyle was dead.

5   DRIVING AWAY

I drive awhile, then sleep. It's hard to do more than a few hours of each. But working it that way, from driving to sleep and a few times not sure which exactly I was doing, I make my way back to Tacoma. I am supposed to meet her downtown.

She'd found me, three years later. Written me at a ranch in Wyoming and told me to meet her in Tacoma. Three years later, after everyone died. After she and I had sex.

And I drive knowing I'll meet her. Of course I will.

And of course I know what's happened. What she needs.

It just took a little bit to face it.

5   RETURNING

It was months after Susan had first talked to him, at the docks in Tacoma, that Brian told her his last name. She'd known his last name, had heard it, but didn't realize what it meant till she heard him say it to her.

To her, Brian did not at all seem like one of the four. He was very quiet. He moved very slowly and said very little and when she saw him those first few times outside of school, he did not drink much.

And already it wouldn't matter that Brian's name was Brian Porter. Didn't matter that he wasn't Kyle. Because, already, Kyle was dead. Already, she was pregnant.

And already she was going to die, at twenty-one. The failure in her was already there. But she didn't know that then. It was the only thing she didn't know, there, alone in this place called Tacoma.

She'd have it, that's what she knew, and she'd not tell this Porter and she'd move back to where her father lived. Not with him, but near him, and she'd have it, and make it work and do her best and be done with this place and everyone here, her mother and her aunt and Kyle and her brother and Porter. Brian Porter.

"What happened to Alaska?" she was saying

now, trying not to hit him, trying not to cry.

She hadn't seen him in three years. Now meeting in some motel near downtown.

"You don't get it," she said. "I don't even know you. I never did. And I didn't ever want to."

He kept nodding. The fucker just kept nodding.

Her words were breath and noise. "She is with you or she dies in a foster home, because there is nowhere else to go and what, fuck, what the fuck happened to Alaska, to Kyle, to getting out?"

And he just kept nodding. Sitting in a chair now. Looking at the car seat on the floor near her.

"Why the fuck did he even like you?" she was saying, screaming, walking, and why the fuck was she going to die, why the fuck was she going to die, and she was sitting, lying back, curled up on the bed, now crying and empty and wanting to die, now, ready to die.

When she sat back up it was later, twenty minutes maybe. He was on the floor, sitting near the seat. Not touching her, or smiling, but sitting near her, on the floor.

He was staring at the car seat. "Kyle was my friend," he said. "I'll never know why. But he was."

And he looked up at her. He was horribly still. Still like Kyle had been, and quiet, so quiet, but horribly, and she remembered the stories, the fights, the rest, and she could see it had been true, all of it and more.

And he spoke. "I know," he said. "But I'll make it work."

EPILOGUE

And at night, in the years after, I would think about them, about the four of us together, and I would think about how lots of kids were like us, how lots of kids had done these things, and I would think about that life and about who I'd been and how I felt and I would lie there, at night, alone with my eyes closed, and for those moments I would miss them and us and everything we'd ever done.

Before Susan wrote me. Before that I'd find myself feeling lonely.

Lonely for the sound of a car radio playing loud.

Lonely for a drive down Shuster Parkway.

Lonely for Teddy.

And for Will Wilson. Will Wilson and all of it, the everything that could happen with him. The purpose and point and moments without time and all that mattered, all that was, all that would ever be.

I had a broken arm and a few cracked and bruised ribs from the wreck, but otherwise I was fine. I didn't even have any scars. Although, for months after the wreck, the smallest bits of glass would appear below the surface of my skin, a tiny edge flashing white in my arm or forehead. And I would pick the bits out easily and carefully flick them away.

No one but family came to Coe's funeral. The same at Teddy's. I stood aside, away from the parents. Coe's parents wanted to blame me. Me more than Will Wilson. Me more than Teddy. They yelled at me as they left the funeral home, swearing and hysterical, his mother trying to grab my arm.

And, in a way, I understood. I was the only one left to hear it.

At Teddy's funeral, his parents both hugged me. I'd known them since I was five. They said very little. But they smiled slightly and stood with me a moment. Still so oblivious to all that we'd done. Three years later, after Susan, they sent me five thousand dollars. Teddy's money. He'd been saving it for college, they wrote later in a note. It was his savings from work. They wished me good luck. Said they knew I would work hard. Said they knew I would do well.

Teddy would want this, they wrote.

And I sat in my bedroom and cried.

People did show at Will Wilson's funeral. Students from school. Maybe twenty, even thirty. Coming in pairs. Many alone. I recognized faces. Knew some by name. But there were kids at Will Wilson's funeral who I'd never seen. Kids who'd simply come to watch. Kids who'd come because of who Will Wilson was.

Only a few people said anything to me. But every one who did speak said, Sorry.

Mr. and Mrs. Wilson were there. Mrs. Wilson crying quietly. Mr. Wilson patting her shoulder.

And Jodi was there. Sitting in the back row alone. Wearing a black jacket and jeans, white t-shirt and sunglasses. She saw me at the graveside, stared at me even when the service was done. People had begun slowly moving toward the parking lot, walking carefully through the headstones. And Jodi stood blankly staring at me.

She was still staring when I finally turned away.

I don't know who would have come to my funeral. My dad and his brothers. My cousins, I suppose. But, back then, before Susan found me, I did hope the curious would have come. Like they'd come to Will Wilson's funeral.

Because in the years afterward, I would begin to convince myself that I'd chosen to end that life with Will Wilson, Coe and Teddy.

And then Susan wrote and I knew all that was a lie.

I don't know what would have happened if the three of them had lived. I sometimes think that it would have gotten worse. That someday we would have pushed too far. And, finally, gotten caught.

Although, other times, I think to myself that we would have gotten jobs on the Tide Flats. Gotten apartments and houses.

I did not grab that steering wheel when I was supposed to. When Will Wilson expected it. But I only sometimes think that I killed the three of them. I think instead about Teddy staring, about how he'd given up and said no, how he'd wanted anything except to continue. And in that moment I considered those things, too. Considered how maybe the only way to end this was to let the car hit the wall. Knocking Will Wilson from the roof. Killing the rest of us, too.

In that moment, I'd seen what we were doing, understood it completely. Cared that it was wrong. But I do always remember that I did reach for the wheel. I did try to steer us away from the wall. I did try to make that life, that night, that moment continue.

I probably only failed because I'd had so much to drink.

And as I drove south from Tacoma, having met Susan and then left, I drove now back to Wyoming, and the job there, and now a child, and I could hear the humming of the car, the wheels thumping quietly across the road. I drove thinking about Kyle.

Kyle grouse hunting. Kyle making dams. Kyle in Alaska.

Alaska was possible.

Sunlight shining on the hood of the car, the car humming steadily along the bright highway.

Alaska was possible. Kyle knew it. He was right.

I've never gone back to Tacoma.

And so that day I met Susan, it was my last time there. Driving in the rain with the windows down but the heat on, pouring warm air into the back seat as I drove across the North End, through Old Town, across the Narrows Bridge, past the smelter smokestack, through downtown to the Tide Flats, out to the Browns Point lighthouse. And then

I drove alone down Shuster. Driving along the high concrete wall, looking up through the rain on the windshield, seeing the wet trees and brush on the hillside, leaning farther forward to try and get some glimpse of the huts. In that last day, I stopped the car only once. Only there on Shuster Parkway. Only there where Will Wilson's car had landed. Getting out of the car in a stretch of dirt beside the road, the cars beside me speeding fast, their tires cutting sharply through the puddles on the pavement. Some drivers maybe seeing me, absently glancing at a car on Shuster, barely noticing the seat in the back as they turned their eyes to the road, forgetting already this long-haired kid in a sweatshirt walking slow circles in the shadows of the gulch.

ERIC BARNES

Eric Barnes is the author of the novel, *Shimmer* (Unbridled Books 2009), and has published numerous short stories in *Prairie Schooner*, *The Literary Review*, *Best American Mystery Stories*, and other publications. He lives in Memphis with his wife, Elizabeth, and their four children. He is also the publisher of *The Daily News*, *The Memphis News* and *The Nashville Ledger*.

CPSIA information can be obtained
at www.ICGtesting.com
Printed in the USA
LVOW11s1427220218
567551LV00002B/115/P